"April, I'm not—"

"Try it. You might like it." She slowly transferred the baby to him.

"Stay right here so nothing bad happens." Ryker accepted the tiny girl with reluctance but he did take her.

"Nothing bad will happen. Isn't she sweet?"

He stood very still, his breathing unsteady as he cradled the baby in his arms and looked down at her, his expression dazed. "There's nothing to her. She's...like a baby bird."

"She is, a little bit, with her hair sticking up like that." Her voice wavered and she hoped he wouldn't notice.

She'd made a mistake encouraging him to hold this child. The image of him clutching a tiny baby to his massive chest would haunt her. She'd imagined it so many times when she'd been desperately in love with him. Now here he was standing before her, the embodiment of her teenage fantasies. But the baby wasn't theirs.

A COWBOY'S RETURN

THE MCGAVIN BROTHERS

Vicki Lewis Thompson

Ocean Dance Press

A COWBOY'S RETURN
© 2017 Vicki Lewis Thompson

ISBN: 978-1-946759-15-3

Ocean Dance Press LLC
PO Box 69901
Oro Valley, AZ 85737

Cover art by Kristin Bryant

Visit the author's website at
VickiLewisThompson.com

Want more cowboys? Check out these other titles by Vicki Lewis Thompson

The McGavin Brothers
A Cowboy's Strength
A Cowboy's Honor
A Cowboy's Return

Thunder Mountain Brotherhood
Midnight Thunder
Thunderstruck
Rolling Like Thunder
A Cowboy Under the Mistletoe
Cowboy All Night
Cowboy After Dark
Cowboy Untamed
Cowboy Unwrapped
In the Cowboy's Arms
Say Yes to the Cowboy
Do You Take This Cowboy?

Sons of Chance
Wanted!
Ambushed!
Claimed!
Should've Been a Cowboy
Cowboy Up
Cowboys Like Us
Long Road Home
Lead Me Home
Feels Like Home
I Cross My Heart
Wild at Heart

1

Ryker McGavin paced the small terminal of Eagles Nest Airfield while he waited for his passenger to arrive. He'd rather take enemy fire than accept this job, but there was no help for it. April Harris needed a ride up to Kalispell ASAP. At the tail end of the tourist season the other pilots who subcontracted with Joe's outfit, Wings Over Montana, were booked.

If only he'd had a chance meeting with her in town, today wouldn't be so awkward. He'd been back at Wild Creek Ranch for three weeks and had made several trips into Eagles Nest. He'd seen almost everyone else he knew, but he'd never bumped into her.

Eleven years was a long time to go without seeing the woman he'd practically been engaged to. Eagles Nest wasn't very big and passing her on the sidewalk or in the grocery store aisle would've been so much better. They could've traded pleasantries and gone about their business. She likely wasn't thrilled about this enforced proximity, either.

Movement outside the terminal's glass door caught his attention. *April.* His heart beat so fast his ears buzzed. Pushing open the door, she shoved her sunglasses to the top of her head and walked toward him. He'd forgotten how short she was, only five-two. She used to like that he could pick her up without breaking a sweat. He was breaking one now.

She didn't look much different—jeans, sandals, t-shirt, and a backpack over her shoulder. Still beautiful. Her brown hair was in a ponytail like he'd seen hundreds of times and the beaded earrings looked familiar. But her unsmiling expression sure was different. She used to light up with a big old grin the minute she saw him. Then again, he used to do the same.

He cleared the nervousness from his throat. "Hello, April."

"Hey, Ryker." Her brown gaze held his for a moment and skittered away. "It's good seeing you again." She seemed as uneasy as he was.

"Same here."

"Thank you for taking me today. I know it was last-minute."

So polite. So careful. So not the way she used to be with him. "No problem." His chest was tight as he gestured toward the terminal's rear doors. "Out this way. Joe said you're in a hurry."

"Leigh's going to have her baby any minute. I need to be there."

He held the door for her. "She's still in Kalispell, then?" He caught a whiff of her scent. Damned if it wasn't the same citrusy stuff he remembered.

She talked fast, like people did when they were nervous. "That's where she met her husband

John and they both love it there, plus they like being near my folks." She matched her strides to his as they crossed the tarmac headed for the twin-engine Beechcraft. "But it's just like Leigh to have her baby on the same weekend as the fair. I was incredibly lucky there were any rental cars left."

"Glad you got one."

"Is that the plane?"

"My plane." The Beechcraft was older than he was, but solid.

"You own it?"

"Me and Badger."

"Who?"

"My Air Force buddy."

"His name's Badger?"

"No, but that's what he likes to be called. He's not out of the service yet, but he wanted a financial stake in the business. That's why I call it *Badger Air*." The logo, a badger wearing goggles and a leather helmet, stood out nicely against the white paint job.

"That's quite a name for an airline."

"He gets a kick out of it." He opened the right-hand door for her. "I can stow your backpack."

"Thanks." She lifted it off her shoulder. "Let me take something out, first." She unzipped a compartment and pulled out two smooth stones, one clear and the other light green. She'd been into crystals when they'd been going together. After tucking them in her jeans pocket, she handed him the backpack and climbed into the co-pilot's seat.

He secured her pack, rounded the plane and swung into the cockpit. Settling into the pilot's seat was an ongoing thrill. *His plane*. Well, his and Badger's. The main thing was it didn't belong to the US government and he could fly in boots, jeans and a t-shirt instead of a government-issued flight suit. His straw cowboy hat, the flea market find his squadron had given him, was stashed behind his seat. He never took off without it.

He buckled up and reached for his headset. "Ever been in a small plane before?"

"No, I haven't."

"I have earplugs if you want them. It gets loud, especially on takeoff."

"Thanks, but I'm sure I'll be fine."

"All righty, then. Let's get 'er done." He put on his headset. "Clear props." When he started the engines, she took a deep breath.

That deep breath was a dead giveaway that she wasn't fine. Could be the flight that rattled her. More likely it was him. Not much he could do about it either way. He kept his focus tight until they were airborne.

How he loved this part, gliding like an eagle over Montana's dimpled terrain. He missed the adrenaline rush of the F-15's speed but he didn't miss being shot at.

Normally at this point in the flight, assuming all was going smoothly, he'd take off the headset and chat with his passenger. Today the weather was clear and air traffic was light. Should be an easy trip to Kalispell.

He slid a glance in April's direction. She looked as miserable as she used to whenever they'd had an argument in his truck—jaw locked, shoulders hunched, hands clenched in her lap. She didn't seem open to conversation.

He could leave on the headset and let her battle her demons. If she'd never been in a light plane before she wouldn't know he was free to talk now that they were on their way. But if she spent the entire flight balled up like that she'd have a headache for sure by the time they landed.

He hung the headset around his neck and looked over at her. "So how've you been?"

She turned to him and blinked. "I...um...good. I've been good. Don't you have to like, fly the plane?"

"I'm flying it. If we maintain altitude and the gauges hold steady, it's all good."

"This must be pretty easy after..."

"Calmer, anyway." If she couldn't bring herself to mention what he'd been doing for all these years, then they needed to talk about something else. "How come I haven't seen you around? I kept thinking I'd run into you in town."

Her cheeks got pink, like they always did when she was agitated, and she started talking fast again. "I've been crazy busy. Geraldine's client list goes on forever, not to mention spending one day a week at the hospital. Leaving so abruptly will cause a scheduling nightmare but I'll deal with it." She seemed to run out of gas at that point but her shoulders had dropped a little.

"Geraldine. Why does that name sound familiar?"

"She's the massage therapist I shadowed our senior year. I've taken over for her."

"Oh." Senior year. Ancient history. Their history. "I didn't know that." His mom had mentioned that April had been back for several months, as if to warn him that he might see her in town. But his mom hadn't elaborated and he hadn't asked questions. "I remember how much you admired Geraldine. I'm not surprised you became a massage therapist."

"I'm not surprised you're flying planes for Joe."

"Did you know I was working here when you called him?"

"Yep. I wondered if I'd get you."

"And here I am."

She didn't comment.

So maybe that would be the end of their interaction. He debated putting the headset on again because the phrase *comfortable silence* didn't apply to this episode. He might as well pretend to be busy flying the plane.

"How's your mom?"

He left the headset where it was. "Good. Pretty much healed." Back in June when he was still deployed, she and his brothers had chosen not to mention that she'd broken her leg when a horse named Licorice had thrown her. They'd meant well, thinking they'd spare him the worry, but it still ticked him off that he hadn't known.

"I was hoping she'd contact me for massage therapy while she was recovering, but..."

"Yeah, well." His mom might have considered that a betrayal of sorts. To be honest, he might have, too. "She's managing fine, now."

"Good." Her shoulders had dropped a little more and her jaw wasn't so tight. "I can't imagine Kendra staying down for long."

"Me, either." He figured she'd started down this conversational bunny trail so he'd follow her there. "Are your mom and dad doing okay?"

"They love Kalispell." Her face relaxed into an almost smile. "They've always wanted some land and they were able to buy a place on five acres. The hospital has several innovative programs and they're pushing for more. Eagles Nest is so small that the resources are limited."

"So why did you come back?"

"Geraldine asked me to. There are several good massage therapists in Kalispell but she was the only one in Eagles Nest. Since she planned to leave, I felt I was needed here."

Her idealistic nature had been one of the reasons he'd fallen for her. She had principles. In the end, that's what had made her break up with him. "I'll bet a lot of folks were happy about that."

"I hope so." She was quiet again.

He was willing to end the conversation there, on a positive note. No hand grenades had been thrown. He still didn't have a lot to do regarding the plane, but he could act like he did.

Except she was looking at him as if she wanted to make a comment.

Finally he turned to her. "What?"

"You seem to have made it home in one piece."

Ah. Did she want to talk about his time in the service, after all? He wasn't sure how to respond. Then he heard Badger in his head, joking around as usual. "If you don't count the prosthesis, the lung transplant and the skin grafts."

"What?"

"Kidding."

"Don't kid about things like that, Ryker. It's not funny."

"Sorry. My sense of humor is more twisted than it used to be."

"I can tell."

He regretted making the joke. Badger would've laughed his ass off but he wasn't with Badger today. Instead of lightening the mood, he'd darkened it.

April tightened up again and her hands were clenched as if she might be holding something. Maybe her two stones.

His fault. He should extend an olive branch. "I noticed you brought crystals along."

"Uh, huh." She opened her hands.

Sure enough, one rested in each of her palms. "What are they?"

She held up the clear one. Her nails were short and unpolished, which made sense for a massage therapist. "This is for safe journeys."

"Appropriate. How about the green?"

"It promotes harmony."

"Hm." Didn't take much to figure out why she'd brought that one.

"I take it you're still skeptical about crystal energy."

He was, but soldiers had talismans they took on a mission to ensure success—baby shoes, garters, snapshots. Even his straw cowboy hat had become a good luck charm, which was why it would go on every flight from now on. He'd be a damned hypocrite if he dismissed her belief in the power of crystals.

He settled for a cliché. "Whatever works."

"Crystals work for me."

"Then would you say we've achieved harmony in this cockpit?"

"Compared to what I thought this trip might be like, I'd say yes, we have."

He gazed at her. "Maybe it's good that we ended up sharing this ride. Maybe we can—" The plane jolted, throwing him against the shoulder harness. "Back to work." The plane hit another updraft and bounced. He put on his headset and looked over at April. "How are you with turbulence?"

"You mean do I have motion sickness?"

"Right."

"Not in a big plane. But this is—" She gasped when another updraft caught them. "This is way more intense."

He reached behind his seat. "Barf bag if you need it."

"Thanks. I'll do my best not to use it."

"Don't be embarrassed if you have to. Lots of people get airsick in small planes." He should probably thank his lucky stars for the updrafts. He had to be careful or he was liable to say something stupid like *maybe we can be friends*. It sounded so evolved to say that, but he couldn't be friends with April. She still stirred him up and that made him vulnerable. Her rejection eleven years ago had sliced deep. He refused to go through that kind of pain again.

* * *

April was *not* going to throw up in Ryker's plane. Tucking her stones in her pocket for safekeeping, she leaned back in the seat, closed her eyes and took several slow breaths. She'd mastered a bunch of relaxation techniques and she'd use every last one if necessary.

"You're better off keeping your eyes open."

"I am?" There went all her techniques down the drain. "Why?"

"I don't know the technical explanation, but focusing on something like the horizon or some other stationary point keeps you from getting disoriented. It seems to calm your stomach, too."

She sat as straight as possible but it was no use. "I can't see the horizon."

"Oh. Sorry about that. You need a booster seat."

"Hey! Be nice!"

"I wasn't teasing you. It's my fault that you can't see out the windshield. If I'd stopped to think about it, I would have brought an extra cushion for you."

"You probably had other things on your mind. You—" She squealed as the plane dropped and then lurched upward again. "Are we okay?"

"We're fine. Updrafts are common in the summer, especially over the mountains. Just find something else to focus on, something inside the cockpit."

His straightforward speech convinced her the plane wasn't about to flip over and crash. When Ryker got scared, he stammered. Not many people knew that because he covered his fear with a glare that convinced people he was furious.

But if she didn't find a focal point and concentrate on it, she might humiliate herself by upchucking. She searched the cockpit. Yes. That. She'd been curious ever since seeing Ryker in the terminal.

He hadn't been inked before he left for the service but now he had a tribal armband. His white t-shirt sleeve partially covered it, but when he flexed his powerful muscles while he guided the plane through the turbulence, the material shifted and she got a better view.

If anything could distract her from this roller coaster ride, Ryker's tattoo should do the trick. The guy's bicep rocked an armband. When he'd been a linebacker for the Eagles Nest High School football team, he'd intimidated every other school in their division with his six-four frame and impressive muscles. During his years in the military he'd doubled down on that impressive physique.

"You holding up okay, April?"

"Yes, thank you." She was into the zone, captured by the arresting combination of tanned skin, toned muscle and a beautifully executed tattoo. Ryker was there in every line of it—the Celtic warrior's knot, the jagged mountain peaks and the eagle in flight. Her heart stirred with a longing she hadn't allowed herself to feel in a very long time.

"We should smooth out pretty soon. That section can be a bad patch. I thought about warning you beforehand, but I could've done that and then nothing would have happened."

"So you fly to Kalispell often?" The ride was still bumpy so she kept her attention on his armband. Making conversation helped, too.

"I haven't been at it long, so I can't say that, but the other pilots go there a lot in the summer. Folks come to Eagles Nest for its small-town Western atmosphere and then head on up to Glacier. Some drive, but enough want to fly that it keeps Joe's operation hopping."

She leaned closer, tempted to run her finger over the design. Bad idea. He must have shaved recently because she could smell his pine-scented cologne. "Was this always your game plan? To work with Joe?"

"More or less. But first I had to check with Mom and see if she needed me at the ranch."

"I take it she doesn't." The play of muscles enhanced that tattoo like nobody's business. She curled her hand into a fist to keep from stroking his arm.

"She has it handled. Zane's still working at the stable full time."

"I heard he and Mandy are getting married."

"Yeah, never saw that coming, but I'm happy for them. Naturally Mandy helps at the ranch sometimes. Then they hired Faith when Mom broke her leg and now Cody's back home. He and Faith—well, that's a long story but those two hit it off. They're putting up a little A-frame in the trees about a half-mile from the house. It's near enough to completion that they can actually live in it."

"Sounds like plenty of people to keep the operation going, then."

"That's what Mom said. Ah, there we go. Should be smooth sailing the rest of the way."

She straightened immediately. Her face had been inches from his arm, but he'd been concentrating on doing his pilot thing so he probably hadn't noticed.

He hung the headphones around his neck again and looked over at her. "What do you think?"

"About what?"

"My armband."

Then he'd been aware of what she was doing, after all. Her face heated. "I needed something to focus on and I picked that. It was more interesting than anything on the instrument panel."

"But do you like it or not?"

The truth popped out. "It's awesome."

He smiled, the first time since they'd met in the terminal. "I think so, too. I found a talented artist who understood what I was looking for. She did a great job."

"She sure did. It looks recent."

"I got it about six months ago. So many of the guys have ink and urged me to do it, but I had to wait until I had my concept and somebody who knew what a Celtic warrior's knot was. The mountains were going to be fairly easy and most people know what an eagle is supposed to look like."

"But not everyone can execute all that and combine it into a cohesive design. It's gorgeous." He would never know about her tattoo, let alone see it. But she'd also found a talented artist and she loved the result.

"My dad had a leather cuff with a Celtic warrior's knot pattern on it. I asked about it years later and found out my Mom had buried it with him. I thought of having one made and then decided this was better."

"I think so, too." They'd been so close their senior year—making love, sharing secrets, but she'd never heard about the leather cuff. "With a tattoo you can work in so many other elements, like the mountains and the eagle."

"This eagle was super important." He glanced down and rubbed his finger over the image. "I was born in Eagles Nest. Then Zane got into raptor rehabilitation so that was another layer of significance. As if that wasn't enough, I've been flying F-15 Eagles practically my entire career."

An involuntary shudder caught her by surprise. The Celtic warrior's knot hadn't freaked her out, maybe because it was an ancient symbol. And she loved eagles. But thinking of him in the cockpit of a jet fighter chilled her blood. He was here and alive, but she'd had way too many nightmares in which he was shipped home in a box.

"That sure was a conversation stopper." He sighed. "Sorry. I know how much you hate...hang on. Hm." He focused on the instrument panel.

"What?" She leaned toward the instrument panel as if she could figure out which of those confusing dials had captured his attention.

"Tell you in a sec." He'd put on the headset again.

"Ryker, what is it?"

He glanced at her. "I don't want you to panic. I can handle this."

"Handle what?" Her stomach churned and she grabbed the barf bag just in case.

"Looks like we're gonna lose an engine."

She threw up into the bag.

2

Ryker hated like hell to upset her, but she wasn't an idiot. When the right engine stopped working and he had to put all his energy into flying the plane, she'd know they had problems, especially if she looked out the window and noticed the propeller wasn't turning.

She'd stopped retching so he lifted his butt off the seat, pulled a bandanna from his back pocket and handed it to her.

"Thanks."

"Welcome."

"It's comforting that you still carry a bandanna."

"It's a cowboy thing."

"Will it fall off?"

"What?" He kept his attention on the fuel pressure as the right engine sounded a death rattle. He'd moved into the familiar state of hypervigilance that had been his salvation during all those hours of aerial combat.

"The engine." She gulped. "You said we'd lose it."

"It'll just quit. The fuel pump's gone out. Fortunately, it's the engine on the starboard side, which is less critical."

"That's the one near me, isn't it? I hear it struggling."

"Don't worry. We can make it on one engine."

"Won't we fly in a circle?"

Despite the tense situation, he smiled at her conclusion. It was perfectly logical if not aeronautically correct. "Not if I can help it." She needed something to do, though. "Still got your safe travel crystal?"

"In my pocket."

"Well, get it out."

"Excellent idea." Her voice sounded stronger, more ready to face this challenge.

"And grab my hat. It's behind my seat."

She leaned over. "Got it. Are you going to wear it?"

"Won't work with my headset. I was thinking you could put it on."

"Why?"

"It's my lucky hat."

"All right, then."

"Thanks." From the corner of his eye he watched her take down her ponytail so she could put on the hat. Yeah, that had been the right move. She was breathing normally again.

She looked over at him. "We'll be fine."

"Absolutely." He felt the engine go. "Okay, April. Get that crystal working. Next stop, Kalispell."

He blocked out everything except the task at hand. He sweet-talked that Beechcraft into cooperating and she responded like the valiant aircraft she was. By the time he was in radio contact with Glacier International, his t-shirt was soaked through. He apprised the tower of their situation, said a little prayer and activated the emergency hydraulics. The landing gear and the flaps came down on schedule. Hallelujah. Forty-three minutes and twenty-two seconds on one engine. He'd prefer not to do that again.

The landing was far from perfect, but he sighed with relief as he taxied past the emergency vehicles parked beside the runway. Wouldn't need 'em.

The ground crew directed him to his tie-down. Switching off that hard-working port engine, he removed his headset and turned to April. "We did it."

"You did it." She looked a little pale and shaky, but basically okay.

"Team effort. You had that crystal."

"And you. I had you." There was a bit of hero worship in her expression.

In any other context, they would have bonded over this experience. But years of pain couldn't be wiped out just because he'd brought the plane in for a safe landing. "You need to get to your sister."

Her eyes widened as if she'd just remembered why she was sitting in his plane. "Leigh. I need to call and see what's happening. My phone..."

"Is probably in your backpack."

"It is."

"Let's go. You can make your call once we're in the terminal." He climbed out and spoke briefly with the ground crew before grabbing her backpack and escorting her into Glacier Jet's facility. He'd been here a couple of times and had been impressed with how well the staff treated everyone, from the high rollers flying private jets to guys like him with a thirty-year-old Beechcraft.

The maintenance crew could fix his plane, but the terminal was busier than he'd ever seen it. The Northwest Montana Fair and Rodeo had been a big deal when he was a teenager. Logically it had grown since then. He'd likely be stuck here for a few hours, if not longer.

He glanced at April. "While you make your call, I'll ask how soon they can replace my fuel pump."

"It's already past five. I can't believe you'll get out of here tonight."

"We'll see. I'll be back."

"Want your hat?"

"Keep it for now."

"Okay." She plopped into a chair. "I'll be right here."

It didn't take him long to find out that the maintenance crew had its hands full. With luck, they could check out his plane in the morning but they couldn't guarantee he'd be able to fly out tomorrow. He returned to the spot where he'd left April.

She was on her feet, pacing as she talked on the phone. His hat looked damned cute on her. He should get it back. He couldn't afford to be charmed.

She glanced at him as she continued to talk. "I'll get there as soon as I can. Right. I'll let him know that." She disconnected the call. "What did they say?"

"That they couldn't get to it until morning."

"With all the activity around here, that makes sense."

"You said you'd booked a rental. If you'd be willing to drop me at a hotel on your way, I can—"

"You'll be lucky if any hotel or motel has a vacant broom closet. I figured you'd be stuck here overnight and Mom invited you to stay at their house."

"Uh, no, that's okay." He glanced around the terminal to evaluate potential sleeping space. A row of three armless chairs might work. "I'll just hang out here."

"That's a terrible idea."

"Seriously, I don't want to put your folks to any trouble." *Or get any more enmeshed in your life.*

"It's no trouble. They have two extra bedrooms now that Leigh and I have moved out. If you try to wedge yourself on those chairs, you'll be crippled by morning."

"Not necessarily."

She sighed. "Yes, you will. Besides, Mom is grateful that you brought me up here and wants to offer you a place to sleep."

"But—"

"It's the sensible solution, Ryker. Come with me and stay with my folks. Please."

She was right about the chairs and his reluctance was beginning to sound like paranoia, cowardice or both. Her parents had always been nice to him. He hadn't seen them since the breakup, but they'd invited him to stay and refusing would border on rudeness. "All right. Thank you."

"You're welcome." She took off his hat. "Here you go, cowboy."

That simple phrase hit him in the gut. She used to call him cowboy all the time when they were going together. Then, because fate could be cruel, his squadron had decided to nickname him Cowboy.

They'd been determined about it. He was from Montana and could ride and rope, so the nickname made sense to them. But every damned time they'd called him that he'd thought of April.

She headed for the rental car counter and he followed. She probably had no idea she'd landed a body blow and she wouldn't find out, either. He put on his hat and tugged down the brim. He could tolerate anything for a few hours. Tomorrow morning they'd fix his Beechcraft and send him on his way.

Twenty minutes later he wedged himself into the passenger seat of the tiniest car he'd ever had the misfortune to ride in. His hat brushed the headliner so he took it off. Even with the seat all the way back his legs were crunched.

"It's all they had." April gave him a look of sympathy as she put her hair back into a ponytail. "I know you're squished."

"It's only temporary."

"Thank goodness." She put the car in gear. "You're okay with going straight to Leigh's house, right?"

"Sure, but shouldn't we go to the hospital if she's already in labor?"

"She isn't at the hospital." She pulled out into traffic.

"Why not?"

"She's having her baby at home, with a midwife."

"She is?"

"You sound shocked."

"I just...it never occurred to me. I thought we'd be going to the hospital." Where he'd sit in the waiting room, call his mom to let her know he wouldn't be home tonight, and read whatever magazines they had lying around until the baby was born. He wouldn't have had to participate in any of it.

"Leigh and John always planned on a home birth unless complications developed. Mom said everything's proceeding as it should."

"So she'll have the baby...where? In their bedroom?" The idea made his stomach churn.

"I'm pretty sure that's the plan, although she could set up anywhere in the house because she's using a birthing stool."

"I have no idea what that is." And he didn't care to learn. If it turned out that Leigh was having that baby in the living room he'd tough it out in this sardine can of a vehicle rather than go into the house.

"There are several different designs, but a stool allows a woman to give birth in a squatting position instead of lying on a bed. It's an old technique that's coming back into favor."

He let out a breath. "I see."

"My dad and John are registered nurses so they'll be monitoring the situation. They—oh, Ryker, poor guy. You should see your face."

"What about my face?"

"Clearly you're put off by this whole thing."

"It doesn't seem quite safe. But then, I have no experience with babies, let alone having them on stools and such. When my mom brought Cody home from the hospital I thought she'd gone to the baby store and picked him off a shelf. I still cling to that image."

"Hey, I apologize. I'm so happy about this birth and so used to being around people in nursing that I forget not everybody is comfortable talking about the process."

"Not my favorite topic."

"I also might have been guilty of thinking that you'd be different, now. I mean, you've been through a lot..."

"Believe it or not, I never got over being squeamish. Good thing I was a pilot. Didn't have to deal with it as much."

"Then I can see why you wouldn't want to be anywhere near this event."

"I'd rather not." Only a few people knew that he had a queasy stomach. April was one of them. And the sight of blood was his kryptonite. Somehow he'd managed to play high school football and serve in the Air Force with only a couple of incidents. Blood made him faint. She'd never seen him do it, but his brothers said it was like a giant redwood crashing to the ground.

"Tell you what. Leigh and John have a front porch, so you don't have to come in. That will remove the risk that you'd accidentally see something that would bother you. You can sit out there until it's all over. From what my mom was saying it won't be long."

"Then I'll take that option." He relaxed. "Do they know if they're having a boy or a girl?"

"No. They wanted to wait."

At last something he could agree with. "I like that idea."

"I know."

"How do you..." It came to him the minute he started to ask the question. They'd talked about it. They'd discussed how many children was a good number and had settled on two. They'd agreed it would be more fun if they didn't know the baby's sex in advance. They'd laughed about the likelihood that he'd faint in the delivery room and had decided he couldn't be there.

They'd been sitting at the soda fountain in the Pills and Pop drugstore having hot fudge sundaes. Her hair had been longer, almost to her waist. She'd been wearing the light blue sweatshirt he'd given her with the ENHS Golden Eagles logo on the front.

"We're here."

He refocused on his surroundings—the driveway of a one-story house with dark brown shingles and white trim. And a front porch.

She glanced over at him. "That drugstore discussion was a long time ago."

"Yes." But it seemed like yesterday.

"I need to go in." She opened her door. "The porch chairs are comfy. I'll let you know when the coast is clear."

"I don't have to come in at all, you know. I can wait until you're ready to leave."

"You don't want to see the baby later?"

How could he say no to that? "You're right. Sure. I'd love to see the baby."

"Don't worry. I'll make sure there's no blood on her."

"I thought they didn't know what they were having."

"They don't and neither do I, for sure. It's just my auntie's intuition that they'll have a girl." She got out and pulled her backpack from the miniscule rear seat. "See you soon."

She dashed up the front steps, her ponytail swinging. She was excited about Leigh's baby. She'd been excited talking about the babies they'd planned to have, too. She'd seemed eager to be a mom at eighteen and yet she didn't have kids yet. Or a husband. Maybe she'd changed her mind, but whether she had or not was none of his business.

Once she was inside the house with the door closed, he extricated himself from the itty-bitty car and put on his hat. Then he walked around the grassy yard and stretched to work out some of the kinks. His shoulder ached, which was normal after a flight, especially one involving broken fuel pumps and costly repair bills.

The bullet he'd taken three months ago had done a number on his shoulder on its way through. The doctors had predicted he wouldn't be pain-free for a while, at least a year and maybe longer. He hadn't planned to tell his family about the incident but then Cody had punched him playfully in the shoulder one evening and he'd flinched. Now his brothers all knew about it but his mom hadn't been around for either the punch or the reveal. They'd all agreed that news of his injury could wait.

Speaking of his mom, he should call her. Pulling out his phone, he continued to walk around the yard while he waited for her to answer. When she did, he heard eighties music and laughter in the background. "Hey, Mom! Party time?"

"It's Whine and Cheese Club night. Deidre's showing us some new belly dance moves."

He smiled. "Sorry I'm not there to see that." Those five women always had a blast. Three were his mom's high school friends and the fourth was Aunt Jo, Mandy's mom. Aunt Jo wasn't really his aunt but he'd known her most of his life and she'd be officially related once Mandy and Zane got married next month. "Tell everybody hi for me."

"I will. What's up?"

"Had a little plane trouble. I'm staying overnight in Kalispell. Should be home tomorrow."

"What kind of plane trouble?"

"Fuel pump."

"Oh. That should be fairly easy to fix."

"Should be." He was grateful for her ignorance about small planes and fuel pumps. Eventually he'd tell her the whole story, but not over the phone. "Anyway, I'll see you sometime tomorrow."

"Okay. Thanks for calling, sweetie."

"You bet. Have fun."

"You know it. 'Bye."

"'Bye, Mom." He disconnected and sent a quick text to Joe giving him the bare essentials.

Joe's text came back rapid fire. *You da man. Stay alive, K?*

Smiling, he climbed the porch steps and settled into one of the cushioned rattan porch chairs. Wait a minute. Were they playing *music* in there? Yes. And it wasn't his favorite downhome country music, either. His travels courtesy of Uncle Sam had taught him things about other cultures and allowed him to recognize a sitar. He'd been lucky enough to spend a few days in Delhi and sitar music was everywhere in that city.

Also in Leigh and John's home, apparently, while Leigh was in labor. He caught a faint whiff of incense. A midwife, Indian music, incense, a birthing stool—he was *so* relieved to be out on the porch. He and April hadn't been on the same page eleven years ago. Judging from this episode, they were no longer reading the same book.

3

April was eager to see her sister and just as eager to get away from Ryker. Being intimately packed into the car with him after he'd courageously saved the day had awakened some inconvenient urges. She'd distracted her pesky libido by talking about the birthing process. She hadn't meant to shake him up.

She called out a greeting when she walked through the front door.

Her mom emerged from the master bedroom, long silver hair in disarray, her cheeks pink with excitement. "Oh, honey, I'm so glad you made it in time! I just know Leigh is craving a back massage. If you didn't bring your essential oils, then I have—"

"I did."

"I knew you would. The midwife's name is Shelley and she's great. The contractions are about two minutes apart now. I know it hurts but she doesn't want anything for pain. A massage would save the day."

"Then let's do that."

"Where's Ryker?"

"I left him on the porch. He's squeamish about childbirth."

"Then you did the right thing. How was your flight?"

"I'll tell you later."

"Awkward?"

"Eventful. Let's go see my baby sister." She followed her mom into a bedroom filled with the scent of flowers and exotic fragrances from the East. Soothing sitar music poured from John's top-of-the-line speakers.

Leigh sat on the birthing stool with paint cloths underneath to protect the floor. Her dark hair was pulled back with a clip and her beautiful face was shiny with sweat when she glanced up at April. "Hey."

"Hey, yourself, gorgeous." April lowered her backpack to the floor and unzipped it to get out her oils.

The midwife, an olive-skinned woman who looked to be in her mid-thirties, came over. "I just checked her. She's fully dilated. Should be soon."

"We're all hoping." Her dad, the sweetest man in the universe, gave April a hug. He'd started growing a beard and it tickled her cheek.

Then she turned to hug John, the second sweetest man in the universe. He wasn't growing a beard, but his blond hair was long enough to put in a ponytail.

He leaned down to murmur in her ear. "Thanks for coming. She needs you."

"I hope I can help." She'd chosen ylang-ylang and clary sage and had diluted each with a carrier oil so the effect would be gentle. She started with the clary sage, pouring the mixture into her palm and oiling her hands before she stepped over to Leigh and began massaging her lower back.

Leigh moaned. "That's heaven. Keep it up."

"You bet." She alternated between the clary sage and the ylang-ylang mixture and felt Leigh relaxing into the contractions instead of fighting them. "Good job, sis. If you feel like yelling, yell. Let's get this baby into the world."

"Works for me. Turn up the music."

April glanced at John, who raised the volume.

Leigh let loose with a loud wail, then another. "She's coming!"

April backed off and Shelley moved in. The next few minutes passed in a blur that ended with a squalling baby girl.

"I knew it!" Leigh sent John a triumphant look. "Didn't I say that?"

"You sure...you sure did." John could barely speak and his expression was incandescent. "I love you." He supported her with an arm around her waist as they carefully made their way to the bed, which had been prepped with absorbent pads. Shelley followed with the baby.

The midwife neatly handled the afterbirth and the umbilical cord while April's dad and John hovered nearby as if to double-check her work. April got a charge out of that. Technically either of the men could have delivered this child, but they'd decided early on they'd be too emotionally involved to do a good job.

The tiny girl nestled against her mother and began to nurse. Leigh sighed. "Nailed it."

That made everyone laugh, although April wasn't the only one wiping happy tears from her eyes.

Shelley said her goodbyes and collected hugs and expressions of gratitude before she slipped out the door.

April's mom walked to the bed and smoothed a hand over the baby's fuzzy head before leaning down to kiss Leigh's cheek. "Super job."

"Thanks, Mom." Leigh's eyelids were starting to droop. "Thanks to all of you. I have an awesome family."

"And an awesome little girl." April gave her sister a smile and a quick peck on the cheek before stepping back to make way for her dad.

He kissed Leigh on the forehead and glanced at John. "We'll leave you with Leigh and the baby for a little while. If you need us, just holler."

"Thanks." John got choked up again. "For everything."

"Wouldn't have missed it." April's dad gave John a hug before turning toward April and her mom. "Let's vamoose." He ushered them both out the door and closed it behind him.

April walked into the living room and spotted Ryker through the pair of windows that looked out on the porch. He'd tipped his hat down over his face as if he might be napping.

Her dad chuckled. "Looks like your pilot's taking a snooze."

"I see that. Now I can't decide if I should go out there or let him sleep. I'm sure he's exhausted."

"From what?" Her mom peered at Ryker's unmoving form. "Isn't it only a two-hour flight?"

"Yes, but about halfway here one of the engines conked out."

Her mom clapped a hand to her mouth and stared at April in horror.

"Whoa." Her dad looked from the window back to April. Then he cleared his throat. "Guess we have quite a bit to be grateful for today."

"No kidding! Oh, April!" Her mom gathered her close. "Were you scared?"

"Well, sure." She gave her mom a reassuring squeeze and stepped back. "But if it had to happen, at least I had Ryker flying the plane. I figured our chances were pretty good."

Her mom took a shaky breath. "You said he had to stay overnight because his plane needed some routine maintenance."

"I wasn't going to tell you the whole story right then."

"No, of course you wouldn't."

"For all I know, replacing a fuel pump might be considered routine."

"Coming in missing one engine isn't routine," her dad said. "He must be a damned good pilot to have pulled that off."

"He should be. He's been flying F-15s for a bunch of years."

"Even so." Her dad scratched his beard. "I don't want to wake him up if he needs the rest, but I sure as hell would like to thank him for saving the day."

"Keep an eye on him, April," her mom said. "I'll go see what we have to eat around here. The food situation hasn't been what you'd call organized recently."

"I'll help you." Her dad trailed after her mom. "Do we have any booze in the house? We have several things to toast."

April smiled at that. Her dad was big on celebrating good times. As she watched Ryker sleep, her remaining tension slowly drained away. The awkwardness of seeing him again was a blip on the radar compared to a brush with death and the joy of being here when Leigh gave birth. Without Ryker's courage and expertise....

He sat up and shoved back his hat. Then he blinked. Logically she shouldn't be able to detect that through the window, but he had the longest lashes she'd ever seen on a guy. The combo of those lashes and McGavin blue eyes was powerful. She'd fallen hard at sixteen.

She should go out there, but she hesitated. The tension she'd thought was gone came slinking back. A dozing Ryker was less threatening than a fully alert Ryker, especially this version of him—older, more experienced, more intense.

His expression during the critical moments of their flight was burned into her brain. The granite-jawed combat soldier had swung into action today, his eyes glittering with an unholy fire, his mouth set in a grim line of determination. She was unwillingly fascinated...no, not just fascinated. Aroused.

Pulling out his phone, he checked it and shoved it back in his pocket. Then he settled into the chair and repositioned his hat over his eyes as if prepared to go back to sleep. Whether he was threatening or not, she had to go out there. He might be hungry and thirsty and yet he was waiting patiently for her to let him know what would happen next.

He sat up immediately and pushed himself to his feet when she came out the door. "Is the baby okay?"

"She's fine. Beautiful. Everything went perfectly."

"Good." His five o-clock shadow gave him a rakish air. "That's very good news. Guess you were right about Leigh having a girl."

"Leigh thought she would, too."

He nodded. "The baby's probably sleeping, now, right?" He sounded hopeful.

"I'm sure. We left John in there with Leigh and the baby so they could have time alone."

"Great idea." He visibly relaxed.

"I told Mom and Dad about the engine going out."

"Oh. How'd they take it?"

"Naturally they were shocked, but they're also grateful that you got us through it. They're inside rustling up some food. Would you like to come in and eat something?"

"Now that you mention it, I'm pretty hungry. Didn't eat much before the flight."

"I had lunch, but..." Her face grew hot. "We both know what happened to that."

"It's nothing to be embarrassed about. The toughest soldiers you'd ever meet can be hit with motion sickness."

"Kind of you to say so."

"It's true."

The front door opened and her dad came out. "Hey, Ryker." He crossed the porch, arm outstretched. "I'm in your debt. Eileen and I both are."

"Just doing my job, Mr. Harris." He shook her father's hand.

"None of that Mr. Harris stuff. Call me Kevin."

"Force of habit."

"Yeah, well, habits can be changed. Hungry?"

"Yes, sir. I mean, Kevin. Starving, actually."

"Then let's get in the house and tie on the feed bag. Eileen's ready to serve up a tofu and veggie stir fry."

April cringed. Her folks had served him a similar dish years ago and he'd confessed to her later that he'd barely been able to choke it down. He was a meat and potatoes man.

But he reacted with enthusiasm. "Sounds terrific." He held the door while she and her dad went through. Then he took off his hat and glanced around as if looking for a place to put it.

"I'll take it." She laid it brim-side up on the mantle as she lowered her voice. "Are you okay with the meal?"

"Sure, why not?"

"I just—never mind. Let's go eat."

"Our hero woke up," her dad announced as they walked into the kitchen. "And he's starving."

Her mom turned from the stove, hurried over to Ryker and threw her arms around him. "Thank you!"

"You're welcome, Mrs. Harris." He patted her back. "Just doing my job."

She stepped away and smiled. "After saving my daughter's life I think you can call me Eileen."

"I don't deserve credit for that considering I was also saving my own a...skin."

"Well, I choose to give you credit, so there. Plates are on the counter and I'll let each of you dish yourself from the stove."

"We have wine and beer," her dad said. "I know April will take wine, but—"

"Small glass, Dad. I'm driving."

"Yeah, I saw your rental. I can't imagine how you shoehorned Ryker into it."

"It presented a challenge." In more ways than one.

Her dad turned to Ryker. "What can I offer you?"

"A beer would be fine, thanks." He waited until everyone else had taken a serving before spooning a generous portion on his plate and sitting down at the kitchen table.

Her dad raised his wine glass. "A toast to the arrival of our granddaughter."

The round table was small so they could all reach to the center and touch glasses, or in Ryker's case, a beer bottle. It was also small enough that Ryker's knee bumped April's, and if she wasn't careful she'd nudge his elbow. He dwarfed the kitchen chair, too.

Her mom took a sip of her wine. "Her birth was so amazing. I couldn't ask for a better welcome into the world, either."

"I know." April met her mother's gaze. "Think of it. Her first hour of life and she's surrounded with nurturing love. She has Leigh and John, you and Dad, and me. What a foundation to build on."

"That's for sure," her dad said. "No telling what she'll do, but I can't wait to find out."

April nodded. "Me, either. Make way for the next generation."

"The circle of life." Her mom lapsed into a contented silence.

Ryker set down his beer and picked up his fork. "Does she have a name?"

"I think Leigh and John settled on something," her dad said. "But we'd better wait and let them tell us in case I'm wrong. Anyway, I have another toast." He raised his glass. "To Ryker McGavin, who brought his crippled plane in for a safe landing, thus delivering our precious April to us safe and sound."

"Amen to that." Her mother picked up her glass.

April followed suit.

But Ryker left his bottle on the table. "I don't think I'm supposed to toast myself." His color was high. "And like I said, I was doing what I've been trained to do, which is no big deal."

"It's a big deal to us, son." Her dad glanced across the table at a very uncomfortable Ryker. "You don't have to toast yourself. I get that. And I can see that we've embarrassed you, but I want you to understand how much we appreciate what you did."

"But—"

"I don't care that you had other reasons to save that plane besides protecting our daughter. I suspect she was a big part of your motivation, and for that I'm grateful. Here's to you, soldier."

April almost dropped her wine glass. Her pacifist father was addressing Ryker as *soldier*? In a way that was clearly a compliment?

Ryker cleared his throat. "Thank you."

"And now let the poor boy eat," her mom said, "before the food gets cold."

Ryker did eat, cleaning his plate and going back for seconds after her mother urged him to. April could only conclude that during his years in the service he'd broadened his horizons when it came to food. He'd polished off his second helping when John walked into the kitchen. He was not alone. He'd brought the baby.

Everyone stood, but April's mom was the first to make it over to John. "Is everything all right?"

John's smile was weary. "Everything's fine. She ate a little more and I decided Leigh needed to rest without having to worry about her so I brought her out here to see you guys."

"I'm so glad you did. Let me take her." She lifted the baby from his arms. "John, this is Ryker McGavin, the pilot who brought April up here."

"Pleased to meet you." John shook Ryker's hand. "Leigh really wanted April to be here, so I'm glad you were available."

"Me, too."

"Hey, John," her dad said. "Are you hungry?"

"I could eat."

"Oh, man." Ryker sighed. "I finished off the stir fry. Sorry."

"No worries," her dad said. "I'll make him a sandwich. Have a seat, John. You look exhausted."

"I'll admit I'm wiped out." He lowered himself into a chair. "We didn't sleep much last night. But she's here and she's perfect, so that's the main thing." He glanced at April's mom. "But I'm a little worried I might fall asleep tonight when Leigh needs me. Or we'll both be so unconscious we won't hear the baby."

April's mom gazed at him. "Would you like Kevin and me to stay here tonight?"

"Would you? I know you'll have to run home to feed the goats and chickens, but if you'd consider coming back after that—"

"I can feed the goats and chickens," April said. "I can also pick up whatever anybody needs on my way back over here in the morning."

Her dad turned away from the counter where he was slicing a tomato. "Just so it's not bigger than a bread box. That rental's tiny. Maybe you should take your mom's Prius."

She was tempted.

"She'll have extra room in the morning," Ryker said. "She'll be dropping me off at the airport."

John looked confused. "You're staying over?"

"His plane needs some maintenance," April said. She'd tell John and Leigh the whole story later when they weren't emotionally tapped out. "So he's bunking at the folks' house tonight."

"Oh." John seemed to be trying to make sense of it but then he shrugged as if giving up. "Okay."

Leigh's faint voice called from the bedroom and John started to get up.

"I'll go." April's mom handed the baby to her. "Take care of this little sweetie for a minute."

"You know I've been dying to hold her." She hadn't cuddled many newborns but this cherub seemed to fit in her arms just fine. She focused on the baby's unblinking stare. "Hello, little one." Blue eyes, but they might not stay blue. John's were hazel and Leigh's were brown like April's. The little girl's hair was the color of wheat, but that could change, too.

John had her swaddled in a soft blanket but she'd worked one impossibly tiny hand out of the folds. "You are so precious." April offered her little finger and the baby gripped it. "You're one lucky girl, you know that?"

"I'll bet she does."

She glanced up at the sound of Ryker's voice and discovered he'd moved closer. "Want to hold her?"

"Oh, no." He took a step back. "She's brand new. I could louse it up."

"No, you can't. I'll be right here. Have you ever held a newborn?"

"Never. I can't remember the last time I held a baby, let alone one only hours old." Yet he seemed fascinated by the tiny girl.

"Then take this chance to experience it." She closed the short distance between them. "As big as you are, you'll only need one arm."

"April, I'm not—"

"Try it. You might like it." She slowly transferred the baby to him.

"Stay right here so nothing bad happens." He accepted the tiny girl with reluctance but he did take her.

"Nothing bad will happen. Isn't she sweet?"

He stood very still, his breathing unsteady as he cradled the baby in his arms and looked down at her, his expression dazed. "There's nothing to her. She's...like a baby bird."

"She is, a little bit, with her hair sticking up like that." Her voice wavered and she hoped he wouldn't notice.

She'd made a mistake encouraging him to hold this child. The image of him clutching a tiny baby to his massive chest would haunt her. She'd imagined it so many times when she'd been desperately in love with him. Now here he was standing before her, the embodiment of her teenage fantasies. But the baby wasn't theirs.

4

Ryker's plan to maintain a safe distance from April and her family had been ripped to shreds. He'd expected resigned tolerance from her pacifist folks and instead they'd elevated him to hero status. He'd hoped to avoid having any contact with this impending birth and he'd ending up holding the baby. And to his surprise, getting a kick out of doing it.

Worst of all, continued contact with April was eroding his decision to have nothing to do with her. He'd been attracted to her curvy little body since the beginning of their junior year. Time and distance hadn't changed that at all, damn it. Every time he looked at her his groin tightened.

He could have dismissed that as simple lust, but his feelings went deeper than that. He admired her. She was devoted to her family. She'd chosen to do what she loved and was passionate about helping people. They were similar in that way. But they were similar in another, less positive way. Years ago, they'd deeply disappointed each other. They'd gutted their dreams and left them on the banks to dry and decay. There was no coming back from that carnage.

And yet...dear God she was beautiful. After he'd returned the baby to Eileen's capable arms and crammed himself into April's rental for the trip over to her parents' house, he had a chance to observe her at close range. The tiny rental mocked the concept of personal space, which meant he was inches away.

Without trying very hard he could study the curve of her cheek and the delicate shape of her ear. Her handmade beaded earrings swung against the smooth column of her neck whenever she moved her head. That had enticed him at eighteen. It still did.

The scent of her citrus cologne was fainter now, but that allowed her womanly aroma to sift through. He was more worldly than he had been at eighteen, more sensitive to nuances. He wasn't the only one turned on by their proximity in the little car.

After an emotionally charged day, they would be spending the night without chaperones. That was a recipe for disaster. At least he saw it that way. He couldn't speak for her.

"Since when did you start liking tofu and stir fry?"

The question was a welcome distraction. "When you're sick to death of military chow, you start sampling the local restaurants. I spent time in places where they eat stir fry a lot."

"And plenty of veggies."

"That, too." Yeah, they could work this subject for a while. "Are you still vegetarian?"

"Vegetarian and seriously considering going vegan."

"You'd give up ice cream?"

"There are ice cream substitutes."

"I'll bet you can't order a hot fudge sundae at Pills and Pop and ask for an ice cream substitute."

"No, probably not, but it's not like I'd be missing anything. I can't remember the last time I've had a hot fudge sundae at Pills and Pop."

"I can." Damn. Shouldn't have said that.

She flushed. "Now that you mention it, so can I." She gripped the steering wheel a little tighter. "Anyway, I'm glad you could eat my mother's stir fry without gagging."

All righty. They were back on track. "It was delicious. I felt bad about finishing it up when your brother-in-law came in and was hungry."

"Dad handled it. He's the sandwich king. He finds ingredients you'd never imagine would taste good together, puts them in a sandwich and you wonder how you ever got along without that combination."

"But it's all veggies in the sandwich, right?"

"John's vegetarian, too, if that's what you're asking."

"Was he to start with?"

"No, but he eventually decided he liked the concept."

Ryker couldn't see himself taking that road. "I assume your family doesn't eat the chickens we're about to feed."

"You wouldn't, either, once you see them. They're beautiful."

"Beautiful chickens."

"Yessir."

"Are the goats beautiful, too?"

"Handsome."

"And your folks keep these animals why?"

"They've always wanted to. The chickens are my mom's hobby, more pets than anything, although she loves having fresh eggs. The goats are for milk and for amusement value."

"Goats are amusing?"

"If you have to ask, then you haven't spent time with goats."

"That would be a fact." What a nutty idea to have chickens as pets and goats as entertainment. But it aligned with at-home births, sitar music and stir fry. He was so out of his comfort zone. At least he'd had a lot more experience with that after his years with Uncle Sam.

April turned down a lane where the houses sat on acreage. When he saw the turquoise one-story surrounded by leafy green trees, he made a guess it was the Harris residence. He wasn't wrong.

She pulled into the drive. "This is it."

"Colorful."

"Wait until you see the living room." She shut off the motor.

He attempted to get out in time to open her door for her, but it wasn't happening. Working free of that little tin can was like getting a cork out of a wine bottle. He could almost hear the pop as he exited. Or maybe that was his back.

"You really don't fit."

"No, ma'am." He put on the straw hat and adjusted the brim.

"We'll take my mom's Prius tomorrow."

"I'd be much obliged. Here, let me carry your backpack." He'd offered out of habit. He used to do it all the time.

"Thanks, but that's not necessary."

He gazed at her. "Probably not. But it's how I was raised." The sun was setting behind her and the golden glow created a halo of light that made her look like an angel. Once upon a time he would have told her that. His throat tightened. He missed those sweet, innocent days when he'd carried her backpack and they'd believed in a future together.

Her expression softened and she handed him the backpack. "Thank you. That would be nice."

Hoisting the backpack over one shoulder, he followed her up the porch steps to the front door. A small brass plaque hung beside it. While she unlocked the door, he read the plaque—*Peace to all who enter*. Maybe tonight would turn out to be peaceful and calm, but given the circumstances, he seriously doubted it.

The minute she opened the door the tang of incense greeted him. That was trouble. He'd caught a faint whiff of it over at Leigh and John's house, but it was much stronger here, more evocative.

One summer night he and April had risked making love in her bedroom while her family was at the movies. Her house had always been fragrant with incense and the aroma never failed to trigger a memory of that special time with her. It had been their only chance to enjoy an actual bed. Quite likely that same bed was in this house, reserved for when April visited.

As she led him through the living room he recognized some of the furniture. The futon might have a new cushion but the frame looked familiar. The bean bag chairs might be replacements for the ones they used to have, but the round coffee table was the same.

"Mom's in a purple and fuchsia phase." April gestured to the walls.

He stared at the color scheme. Wow. Two walls were a deep pink and the third was the same shade as his favorite seedless grapes.

"Dad thinks it's too intense."

"Can't imagine why."

She smiled. "Mom never sticks with one color scheme for long so he knows it'll change."

"When I read the plaque out front I didn't expect fuchsia and purple walls."

"She just hit fifty. I think that has something to do with it. Go ahead and leave my backpack on the futon. We need to feed the critters."

He set down the backpack and followed her through the dining room and the kitchen without encountering any startling wall colors. Maybe Eileen hadn't gotten around to painting those, yet. She'd always been an interesting woman, full of life much like his mom. Like April, too, for that matter.

The screened back porch was furnished with a wooden table and chairs plus a couple of cushioned lounges. Wind chimes hanging from the rafters tinkled as a breeze came through. Now that was peaceful.

April opened the screen door and hurried down the wooden steps to the yard, but he paused to scope out the situation. Directly in front of him were two thriving vegetable gardens. One was laid out in a labyrinth pattern and the other was in the shape of a peace symbol. No boring rectangles for April's folks.

Beyond that were two large enclosures with six-foot wire fences. The goats were in one along with a miniature barn painted a sedate beige. Some stacked railroad ties gave the goats something to climb on, but they weren't up there now. A small barrel and a couple of dented soccer balls might be toys, but the goats weren't playing with them, either. April's approach had whipped them into a frenzy of bleating and crowding the gate.

An elevated chicken coop sat in the other enclosure. It was fuchsia, probably the same paint as Eileen had used in the living room. From here he couldn't see any chickens because his view was blocked by the veggie gardens.

Descending the steps, he lengthened his stride and caught up with April. "Let me guess. Your dad's in charge of the goats."

"Pretty much, although Mom likes them, too. They've wanted a setup like this for years."

"How do they keep the deer and the rodents out of the gardens?"

"If I tell you, you won't believe me."

"I might."

"At first my dad sprayed the perimeter with products that were supposed to contain predator urine. He had limited success. Then he realized that he was the most dangerous predator of all. Now every few nights in the summer he goes out with a full bladder and—"

"No way." He grinned. "You're making that up."

"See? I knew you wouldn't believe me."

"He really does that?"

"Yep. And it works." She approached the goat pen. "Okay, okay. Settle down, ladies." She unfastened the latch on a waist-high metal bin next to the gate and the bleating intensified.

"What can I do?"

"Hold the pail for me." She handed him a metal bucket she'd pulled from the bin, picked up a scoop and started filling the bucket with pellets. The rattling excited the goats even more.

"Are they used to getting fed earlier?"

She shook her head. "Not really. They're always like this when they know they're about to be fed."

"And your folks think they're amusing?"

"They are when they're not expecting food. You're not seeing them at their best."

"I'll take your word for it." The horses at Wild Creek Ranch liked their evening meal, too, but they didn't carry on like this. Winston might whinny to let everyone know he was hungry, but that was it. Goats didn't seem worth the trouble, but then again, he didn't care for goat milk.

"That should do it." She laid the scoop back in the bin. "I'll take the bucket if you'll get the gate."

He opened it and she slipped inside. He walked in behind her and secured the gate out of habit, but those goats weren't going anywhere. All three were focused on April and that magic dinner pail.

The barn doors stood open and inside were three stalls with a food and water trough in each. April distributed the food. "There you go, Cinderella. Snow White, there's yours. Chow down, Belle. Have a great night, ladies." She left the barn and latched the door. "That's it for the goats."

"Disney princesses?"

"Yeah." As she walked back to the gate, she gave him a teasing grin. "I'm surprised you know that since you grew up with four brothers."

"Four brothers and Mandy. She educated us regarding the princesses."

"True. She would have." April paused and her expression grew wistful. "I'd like to connect with her again, but..."

"You haven't talked with her at all?"

"Oh, you know, briefly if we happen to see each other in town. It's not like she avoids me. Everyone in your family is polite."

But that wasn't the same as welcoming, was it? Now that he'd been treated so kindly by her family, her isolation from his seemed wrong. "I should say something to them."

"No, don't. I understand why they might not want to be friends with me. They're loyal to you. I respect that."

"But we broke up a long time ago. It shouldn't still be a problem. Look at how great your family's been to me."

She held his gaze. "It's not the same. For one thing, they're being nice because you got me here safely. For another, they can afford to be friendly because they live up here. I doubt you'll be seeing them again."

"Guess not." That notion disappointed him, but she had a point.

"Think about it. When you and I are back in Eagles Nest, are we going to be casual friends?"

He took a deep breath. "That would be the best scenario."

"But is it likely? Are we going to meet now and then for a drink at the Guzzling Grizzly? Because that's what casual friends do."

His gut churned at the possibility. He couldn't meet her for a drink and then go home by himself. He'd want...never mind what he'd want. It wouldn't work. "When you put it that way, I can't see that happening."

"Me, either. But it's the kind of relationship we'd need if you expect your family to roll out the welcome mat."

"I guess."

"So let it be with your family, okay?"

"Yeah, okay."

"Let's go feed the chickens."

He didn't like the outcome of that discussion but he didn't have a solution to the issue so he'd have to let it go. And change the subject.

"I'm still trying to figure out why you named the black goat Snow White."

"Hair color. Snow White had black hair, Cinderella was a blond and Belle was a brunette." She put the bucket in the metal bin and led the way over to the chicken enclosure.

"Huh. I wouldn't have thought of that."

"You're a boy. Boys don't focus on hair color the way girls do."

"Sure we do. Most guys have a preference. Zane's partial to blonds. Cody, too." And he preferred brunettes. He halfway expected her to ask but she didn't. Just as well.

"If Zane and Cody like blonds, they would love Marilyn."

"Marilyn Monroe?"

"Marilyn the chicken. Isn't she gorgeous?" She pointed to a chicken strutting around the enclosure.

She was unlike any hen he'd ever seen— fluffy, elegant, with silvery blond feathers. "For a chicken, yeah. I just never thought of chickens as being attractive."

"Then how about Lucy, our redhead?"

"Damn, now there's a pretty chicken." He watched her prance around the yard. "She knows, it, too."

"I think you're right. That glossy black one is Princess Leia. The honey-blond is Dolly and the multicolored one is Lady Gaga."

"No white chickens?"

"Actually there is one with white feathers. She must be hiding. Mom named her Betty White."

"I had no idea chickens could look so different."

"And these aren't as exotic as some." She unlatched a bin like the one for the goats but slightly smaller. "Mom's talked about getting Pekin Bantams, which are even fluffier and come in colors like lavender and blue. But their eggs are small and cream colored. These Easter Eggers lay good-sized eggs in pastels."

"Hang on. Did you call these chickens Easter Eggers?"

"That's their name. After we feed them we'll check the coop for eggs. Then you'll see why they're called that. Hold the bucket while I get their food." She repeated the process they'd used for the goats although the pellets were smaller.

Once again he held the gate while she walked in. Instead of crowding her the way the goats had, the chickens gathered around her in a polite circle, heads bobbing. Their soft little clucks were cute.

She turned to him. "We'll scatter this, so if you want to scoop handfuls from the bucket, you can help."

"Why not?" He was liking these chickens a lot better than the goats. They had manners. They sidled away as he stepped closer and reached into the bucket. "Are we supposed to say anything?"

"You mean like grace?" She sounded amused.

"No, I mean like in the movies when they scatter food for the chickens they say, *here, chickie, chickie, chickie.* Like that."

"You could do it if you want, but we don't have to call them. They're already here. They're right at our feet."

"True."

"I usually throw the food away from me so they'll each have their own little dining area."

"Makes sense. I'll watch how you do it."

"Okay." She took a handful of the feed and tossed it a few feet away.

"Got it." He followed her lead, throwing food as they rotated in a circle without discussing their strategy. They'd always worked well together and that hadn't changed. Cool.

What wasn't cool was his damned shoulder, which had seriously tightened up when he'd been wrestling the plane through the sky. Each time he lobbed a handful of chicken feed, pain stabbed him. He tried not to show it.

"Ryker, what's wrong?"

"Nothing."

"I don't believe you. I'm trained in this and I can see that throwing the seed is causing you discomfort."

"Some." He kept tossing out the seed because it was fun even if it hurt.

"Is it from riding in the rental car?"

"No." Although that hadn't helped.

"Struggling with the plane?"

"That's part of it. It's just a combination of things." A combination that began with crashing an F-15 deep in enemy territory and taking a bullet in the resulting firefight. Thank God for the chopper that had pulled him and his copilot to safety.

"When we get inside I'll give you a massage. That should help."

He panicked. He'd experienced the seductive power of her oiled hands. She used to work him over after every football game and then they'd have sex in the back of his pickup. Once she started massaging his shoulder he couldn't be responsible for the outcome. "I'm fine. No need for that."

"Don't go all macho on me. Between the tense flight and my tiny rental, you've punished your body. You happen to be sharing space with a licensed massage therapist. Take advantage of it."

He tugged his hat lower. "I don't think that's a good idea."

"Ryker, I'm a professional. I can separate my emotional attachment from my work so that I can help you feel better. I'd be shirking my duty if I didn't do that after you made such an effort to get me here."

"We can talk about it once we get inside."

"Fair enough. How are you liking these chickens?"

"Better than the goats."

"The goats will grow on you if you give them a chance."

"I won't be here long enough for that to happen."

"Maybe not. Are you sure you'll get out tomorrow?"

"Don't see why not." He wasn't sure at all, but staying here with her would be tough duty now that they'd agreed friendship was out. That left only one option and that would get him in big trouble.

"Feed's all gone. Let's go check the henhouse for eggs. We could have them for breakfast."

Breakfast was the last thing on his mind. First he had to make it through the night. Her suggestion of a massage dangled in front of him, taunting him with visions of what that massage could be like and where it could lead. To heaven in the short term. To hell eventually.

5

The Easter Eggers came through with a total of six eggs in shades of blue, green and pink. April nestled them in the basket her mom kept hanging on a nail inside the coop and closed the chickens in for the night before walking back to the house with Ryker.

"My mom would go wild for these eggs." He'd been exclaiming over them ever since he'd seen the first one lying in a nest. "Now that she has more help around the place, I'm going to suggest getting a few of those chickens."

"Make sure to critter-proof the henhouse."

"No worries on that score. Remember my little brother Trevor?"

"Of course." The McGavin twins had recently come back from working on a ranch in Texas and she'd seen them a few times in town. Like the rest of the family, Trevor seemed slightly uneasy whenever he talked with her.

"He's working for Paladin Construction, now. He can build that henhouse for Mom if she goes for the idea. I think she will."

"I can picture her raising chickens." Too bad she couldn't help Kendra with it. Or provide her mom's number for more experienced advice. Unless she could magically become Ryker's good buddy, that wouldn't be happening.

The inside of the house was dark as they climbed the steps to the back porch. Dark and way too intimate. She hurried into the kitchen and flipped on a light. It wasn't very bright and she knew immediately why.

"There's a bulb out." Ryker took off his hat and hung it on the back of a kitchen chair. "If you'll get me a new one, I'll change it."

"It's not out, it's missing." She opened the refrigerator and transferred the eggs to a sectioned compartment in the door. "My parents believe in mood lighting to conserve electricity."

"Oh."

"Can I get you something? There's beer. I think it's the same kind you had with dinner, if you liked that."

"It was good, but I'll pass."

"That's fine." She washed her hands at the sink. "I'll fetch my lavender oil so I can massage your shoulder." She was proud of the matter-of-fact way she said it.

"Thanks, but I'll pass on that, too."

"Don't be ridiculous." She dried her hands on a kitchen towel. "Let me work on your shoulder and then you can take a hot shower and go to bed. I guarantee you'll feel better."

"I'll take you up on the hot shower, but I don't need a massage."

She replaced the towel and turned to him. "Give me ten minutes."

"Why are you so determined?"

"Because you're in this condition partly because of me."

"You paid for the flight."

"What you did can't be measured in dollars. And maybe I want to prove to you that I'm right, that I can make you feel better."

His mouth quirked in a half-smile. "That I would believe. But you don't have to prove it. I believe you. Just point me toward the bathroom you want me to use and tell me which bed I'm taking. That's all I need for now."

"Ryker, damn it, I went into this field because I hate seeing people in pain. I get great satisfaction from relieving that pain. Please let me do this for you. Ten minutes."

He glanced up at the light fixture. "Will you have enough light?"

"I don't need light. I'm paying attention to what I can feel, not what I can see. I usually keep the light low when I'm doing a massage, anyway."

"All right, then." He pulled out his phone. "I'll set the timer."

"Wait until I get my oil."

"Where do you want me to sit?"

"If you straddle one of the kitchen chairs so I can easily reach your back, that will work. And take off your shirt."

"Will do."

Hurrying into the living room, she rummaged in her backpack until she found the lavender oil. It was her best option because she wouldn't have to mix it with anything. She didn't want to give him time to change his mind.

But when she walked into the kitchen, she almost changed hers. She'd known he was ripped, but holy hell. Even in the subdued light, the view of his broad back and wide shoulders made her body clench with yearning. *Settle down. Do your job.* "You can start the timer."

He'd laid his phone on the kitchen table. "Starting countdown." He reached over and tapped it.

The movement exposed his right shoulder to more light from the overhead and a blemish on his skin caught her attention. The skin near his scapula was puckered and discolored. She moved closer and stared down at recent scarring that looked exactly like something she'd seen in a medical video during her training. An exit wound. He'd been shot.

She pressed a hand to her stomach and stepped back. "You...you were..." Gulping for air, she turned away and tried to blot out what she'd seen. When the shaking started, she couldn't stop that, either.

His chair scraped the floor as he got up and wrapped his arms around her. "Damn. I thought the light was low enough you wouldn't notice."

"I would have felt it!"

"It's just a scar. No different from getting spiked in a football game."

"Are you serious?" Breathing hard, she whirled away from him. "You were almost killed! How could you get shot? You're a pilot!"

"Planes go down."

Bile rose in her throat. She swallowed and almost choked. "I can't...I'm not..." She put the lavender oil on the counter and shoved past him, heading for the porch and the yard beyond.

"April." His footsteps followed.

"Don't come after me!" Slamming out the screen door, she ran down the steps and into the yard. Then she leaned over, her hands braced on her knees. She expected to throw up, but instead she began to sob.

Stupid, stupid, stupid! Why was she crying? The bullet hadn't killed him. But it could have. And she'd been a damned coward for not facing reality.

Oh, yeah, she'd had nightmares that he'd come home in a box, but had she let herself imagine how he'd end up in one? Had she ever pictured his body crushed in the wreckage of his plane? Or if he'd managed to walk away from the crash, that a blast from an enemy rifle could send a bullet tearing through his flesh?

No. She'd kept her fear at a distance, blocking horrific details with a wall of resentment. He'd *chosen* to put himself in danger. Life was so very precious and he'd agreed to risk his for reasons she hadn't been able to accept. Still couldn't. The violence implied by that bullet wound shook her to the core.

Gradually she became aware that she was walking the labyrinth. She'd made no conscious choice to do it. Around and around she walked until she reached the center where her mother had built a cairn. The small tower of stones calmed her, almost as if her mom were standing there telling her to get a grip.

She'd say it like that, too. *Get a grip, April. It's not about you.* No, it wasn't. Ryker had taken the bullet but she was the one freaking out. She continued circling the labyrinth while she took slow, steady breaths and listened to the crickets. She'd offered him a massage. He still needed one. But she'd be no good to him unless she could knead his poor injured shoulder with gentle compassion.

She'd learned a lot about the human body while studying for this career. No wonder his shoulder bothered him. He was recovering from a bullet wound and would continue to recover for many more months. Wrestling the plane for nearly an hour and then being crammed into her rental had likely inflamed tender tissue.

She'd been granted one ten-minute shot at making him feel better. It wasn't much, but better than nothing at all. And she'd blown it.

At the end of the labyrinth she paused, closed her eyes, and focused on helping Ryker. Then she crossed the yard and climbed the steps to the porch. Light from the kitchen allowed her to see him relaxing on one of the lounge chairs with a beer in his hand. He'd put his shirt back on. Like the mannerly cowboy he was, he got up.

She stood just inside the screen door. "I'm sorry for acting like that."

"My bad. I shouldn't have agreed to the massage."

"Why did you?"

"You really wanted to do it."

"You agreed to please me?"

"Mostly that. But I also knew it would help."

"Oh, really?"

"Before I was discharged, the surgeon who patched me up recommended I find a massage therapist when I got home. I figured I'd need to drive to Bozeman and so I haven't looked into it, yet."

Ah, the irony. Theoretically he shouldn't have to travel to Bozeman. But if neither of them could manage a casual friendship, a therapist-client relationship probably wouldn't work, either.

There was one way to find out, though. "In that case, I'd like to give you that massage. I understand if you'd rather not after the way I behaved, but it would mean a lot to me if you'd agree."

He regarded her silently.

"Ryker, I feel like an idiot for running out of here. I bragged to you about my professional detachment and then I completely lost it. That was humbling. What if I can prove to both of us that I can help you? Then you wouldn't have to drive to Bozeman once a week."

"You'd be my therapist?"

"It would save you time and trouble."

"Time, yes. Not so sure it would save me trouble."

"We could test it now."

He didn't say anything for a while. Then he sighed. "All right. How about doing it out here? It's peaceful and you won't have to look at my scar."

She winced, but that's what she got for overreacting. At least he'd agreed to the massage. "That's fine. I'll get the oil."

He stepped aside so she could walk past him into the kitchen. He took up a lot of space. His massive chest would have been an easy target. But if she expected to succeed with this massage, she'd have to quit thinking about that.

When she came back with the bottle of lavender oil, he'd moved one of the chairs away from the table and was straddling it the way he had before. His shirt was off and he was just as impressive in the shadows as he had been under the kitchen light.

She used to revel in his size and strength. He'd rule the football field, but afterward he'd turn to putty in her hands as she massaged his weary muscles. Eventually he'd get his second wind and she'd be the one melting in the heat of his caresses.

He'd been sexy as a teenager and was twice as sexy now. She couldn't think about that, either. "I'm using lavender oil." She poured a little in her palm and set the bottle on the table.

"I recognized it."

"Oh?" She rubbed her hands together to warm the oil.

"When we were kids, Mom put a drop of it on our pillow if we had a bad dream."

"Good idea." She smoothed the oil over his shoulder. She hadn't expected the rush of pleasure from simply touching him. The texture of his skin was achingly familiar. *Ryker.*

"It worked." He drew in a slow breath and let it out. "Later I did it for the younger ones so Mom didn't have to get up."

That sounded like him. And she was loving this massage *way* too much. She'd have to dial it back. "That was considerate of you."

"She worked hard. She needed her sleep. She still works hard."

"I'm sure she does." She kneaded gently, using mild pressure. His skin had been cool to start with and was growing warmer by the second. Her professional detachment was AWOL but that didn't mean she couldn't help him. When she encountered the ridge of his scar, she imagined her fingers transmitting rays of healing light.

"This is nice."

"I'm glad." She added more oil, using the heel of her hand to coax his tight muscles to relax. She hoped he'd forgotten to set the timer because ten minutes wouldn't be long enough to do a decent job.

"You've gotten better."

"I should hope so." She moved to his other shoulder. That hadn't been part of the plan but unless he told her to stop, she'd keep going. She worked on his neck, too, finding knots and gradually undoing them. Using her knuckles, she moved down the length of his spine to the small of his back, just above where his belt and waistband gapped a little. She slipped both hands into that gap to loosen the tenseness there.

He groaned.

"Am I hurting you?"

"No. Feels good." His breath hitched. "Too good."

"Not possible."

"Yeah, it is." His voice was husky. "You need to stop."

"But—"

"I mean it, April. Back off." He pushed away from the chair, forcing her to move as he turned to face her.

She couldn't see his expression but she didn't have to. His ragged breathing told her everything she needed to know. She'd been fighting her response to him, but if he lost control, so would she. She gulped. "I didn't mean to."

"I'm sure you didn't. You were never a tease. But this experiment is over. It failed."

"I want to help you, damn it!"

"I wish you could. You have magic hands. But I want more than a massage from you and we both know that would be a mistake. Looks like I'll be driving to Bozeman."

* * *

By using every ounce of his willpower, Ryker kept his arms at his sides. He didn't grab April and kiss the living daylights out of her. He didn't take off her clothes and kiss the rest of her until she writhed in his arms and begged him to make love to her. But God, how he wanted to.

Instead he quietly asked her to show him where he'd sleep and where he could take a shower. He'd planned for it to be a hot shower but he'd changed his mind. The cold water pelting his equipment was doing its job when she rapped on the bathroom door and called his name.

He stuck his head out of the shower. "What?"

"You'll need clean undies. These are still in the package. I can buy a replacement tomorrow. I'm tossing them in. And I found some disposable razors, too."

"That's okay. I can —" His protest was cut off when several plastic-wrapped packages sailed into the bathroom and landed on the floor. Then the door closed again.

She'd obviously never known a soldier before. He'd been on missions where he'd worn the same clothes for days and never touched a razor. But he'd be climbing into a bed made up with clean sheets. He could sleep naked the way he always did, but that didn't seem quite right when he was a guest in the house. With April right down the hall.

He couldn't believe what she'd brought would fit him, though. Her dad was six inches shorter and at least fifty pounds lighter. After he dried off he inspected the packages she'd brought. One contained white tube socks. Okay, that would work with his boots. The white t-shirts would be tight and he might ruin one by trying to pull it on. He'd skip that option for now.

The third package contained three pairs of cotton boxers. Was she pranking him or did her father normally wear boxers decorated with green, blue and yellow peace symbols? Because of the roomy style they'd fit okay, but good God. He hadn't worn anything but plain underwear since the Incredible Hulk pair of boxers he'd asked for when he was six.

But he needed something clean to sleep in so he didn't have much choice. She'd said she'd replace everything tomorrow. Could she just walk into any old store and find boxers like these? He had trouble believing it, but then again, he hadn't spent much time in this country recently.

He opened the package, pulled on the boxers and avoided looking at himself in the large bathroom mirror until he'd zipped and buttoned his Wranglers. Apparently, she meant for him to keep this dicey underwear. Oh, he'd keep it, all right. He'd just acquired Badger's Christmas present. He hoped that joker showed up to claim it.

After he'd hung up his towel, he left the razors on the counter so they'd be handy in the morning and carried his stuff into his assigned bedroom. Leigh's old one, most likely. A couple of plush animals, a dinosaur and an owl, sat on the dresser. The walls were pale green and the comforter and curtains were white and lacy. The double bed would be fine. His feet would hang over but he was used to that. This room beat spending the night at the airport and he was grateful.

He'd left his straw hat in the kitchen and he also thought saying goodnight to April would be the classy thing to do now that he'd calmed down. He walked barefoot through the empty living room and into the kitchen. His hat was where he'd left it hanging on the back of a chair, but April wasn't around.

"I'm out here." Her voice drifted in from the back porch.

He went as far as the kitchen door. "Thanks for the underwear."

"How'd you like those boxers?"

"They fit great." If she'd meant them as a joke, he'd pretend not to get it.

"That was the only unopened package in my dad's drawer. I think they're a bit much even for him. I'll bet it was a gag gift from the hospital Christmas party."

"Glad to hear it. I don't picture your dad as the decorated boxer type."

"Yeah, he's not. You didn't finish your beer, by the way. It's probably warm by now, but I left it on the table in case you still want it."

"I've had plenty of warm beer in the past ten years." But he hesitated, torn between his reluctance to waste good beer and his worry about being alone with April in the dark.

"I'm having one if you want to come out for a while before you turn in."

Well, damn, that sounded nice. "I'd like that." He walked out on the porch, the boards smooth under his bare feet. Someone had sanded and varnished them recently.

Picking up his bottle from where he'd left it on the table, he put on his hat and settled down on the vacant lounge chair. The cushion was cool beneath his bare back. The chair was angled in the same direction as April's, but the two were separated by at least five feet. He should be fine.

Or not. Her soft breathing was destroying what the cold water had fixed. Every time she took a sip of beer he relived the joy of kissing her. She put her whole self into it. Maybe he should claim to be tired and clear out.

Then she spoke. "My place in Eagles Nest doesn't have a porch. I miss that. Sitting here and listening to the crickets is nice."

"It is." She hadn't said *sitting here with you* but since she'd invited him to join her, it was implied. He couldn't up and leave after she'd made that comment. They used to enjoy each other's company and not only because of the sex. He had some great memories—horseback rides and picnics in the summer, snowmobiling and cozy fires in the winter. If they went their separate ways after this, which seemed likely, he wouldn't have these private moments anymore. He'd stick it out a little longer for old times' sake.

"I notice you didn't put on one of the t-shirts."

"I was afraid if I tried I'd rip it."

"I thought of that."

"I can wear my shirt on the way home." He took a swallow of his warm beer. "Doesn't matter if I sweated through it today. I'll be the only one in the cockpit."

"You were pretty damp when we climbed out of that plane. You can tell me the truth now that it's over. Did you think we'd make it or were you secretly afraid we'd go down?"

"I knew we'd make it provided I kept my focus. You can't allow yourself to be distracted in a situation like that or you're dead." And there was no way in hell that April Harris was going to die on his watch.

"You were extremely focused. I've never seen you like that."

"We were given excellent training."

"You're glad you went, aren't you? Even though you got shot."

"Yes." A warm breeze ruffled the wind chimes. "But I'm also glad to be home."

"You don't miss the excitement, the thrill of danger?"

"No." He'd always loved the sound of her voice, but she'd broached a loaded topic. She might be looking for closure but he was too jacked up to give her that. If she persisted, she was liable to get either harsh words or hot lovemaking. He polished off his beer and stood. "There's enough danger on this porch to satisfy me. I'm gonna turn in before I get in trouble. Goodnight, April."

6

The rat-tat-tat of gunfire and the whistle of bombs punched Ryker out of a dream and into full alert mode. Damn it, they were hitting the airfield! Had to get those planes up, pronto! He leaped out of bed and reached for his flight suit, but the minute his fingers touched rough denim, he paused. He wasn't in the barracks.

Instead he was standing in a cozy little bedroom in a turquoise house outside the city limits of Kalispell, Montana. Gunfire and bombs made no sense, but fireworks did. The fair would be finishing up for the evening. They were probably capping off the festivities with fireworks.

Adrenaline continued to pour through him, giving him the shakes. No point in trying to sleep until the fireworks were over. Pulling on his jeans, he walked through the dark house to the back porch. Above the trees color bloomed in the night sky. He used to love watching these displays. He took deep breaths and waited for his former childlike delight to slow his heartbeat. He was listening to entertainment, not a prelude to death and destruction.

His brain wasn't communicating with his body. A breeze chilled his clammy skin and he flinched at every boom and crackle. Swearing in frustration, he scrubbed his fingers through his short hair. What an unpleasant reaction to something he'd once enjoyed. Then again, he'd only been stateside for three weeks. By next July, he might be fine. He hoped so, but tonight he hated fireworks with a passion.

He turned away and almost knocked April to the floor. "Whoops!" He grabbed onto her so she wouldn't fall. "I didn't know you were there."

"I heard you get up."

"Yeah, I...the fireworks..."

"Sound like a battlefield?"

"Yep."

"I'm so sorry."

"So am I." He'd let go of her in a minute, but she was so warm and he was so cold. The chill had nothing to do with temperature. She wore a short nightie that left her legs and arms bare but she wasn't shivering.

"Ryker..." Reaching up, she touched his cheek, her tentative caress gentle, caring.

Boom, boom, boom! The finale exploded behind him, hammering at his control. With a groan, he gave up the fight. Pulling her into his arms, he lowered his head and claimed her mouth. Oh, God, yes!

The years fell away. Her lips fit perfectly against his, just like always. She tasted like mint, exactly as she used to. Cupping her jaw, he shifted his angle and deepened the kiss.

With a soft whimper, she welcomed the thrust of his tongue. Then she slid her hands up his bare chest, wound her arms around his neck and held on. He knew this dance. Spanning her waist, he lifted her up and she wrapped her legs around his hips.

The fireworks finale continued, crashing over his head and shoulders. He tightened his hold, craving the heat from her mouth, the heat from her body. When he cupped her ass and settled her against his crotch, she dug her heels into the backs of his thighs to intensify the connection.

His cock rose to meet her hot invitation. She moaned and pressed against him. As she began to quiver with anticipation, he grew steady. The red haze slowly cleared, leaving him sure of one thing. He'd started this and he'd finish it.

Carrying her to the lounge, he straddled it, lowered her to the cushion and followed her down. Then he lifted his mouth from hers and dragged in air. "One question."

She was breathing as hard as he was. "Little raincoats?"

"Yeah."

"Sorry."

"We'll do something else."

"You don't have to—"

"I want to. You can't imagine how much." He gently unlocked her arms from around his neck. "I don't expect to get this chance again." He nibbled at her lips. "I want to hear you come. I want to hear you call my name."

Her breath caught.

"Is that a yes?"

"I never could resist you."

"I never could resist you, either." He leaned into another deep kiss that tasted of surrender. She held his head and kissed him back with enthusiasm, but beneath him, her body relaxed.

When he slipped his hand under her nightgown and cradled her breast, she made a sound deep in her throat, almost like the purr of a cat. He stroked and fondled her silken skin until he needed more. One efficient tug and he pulled the nightie over her head. He tossed it to the other lounge and gazed down at her.

The light was dim, but not so dim that he couldn't see the delicate tattoo against the pale skin of her breast. Over her heart.

Her voice was soft in the darkness. "It's a dove."

"I know." A dove of peace. "When did you get it?"

"The day after you enlisted."

He felt pain in his chest, as if the needles had pricked him, too. "That must have hurt like hell."

She gazed up at him. "I didn't care."

Leaning down, he pressed his lips to the dove. They had such power to hurt each other, even now. He closed his eyes in resignation.

She stroked his hair and her breathing slowed.

Lifting his head, he held her gaze. "I think it'd be better if we didn't—"

"I know."

"I'll take you inside." He levered away from her and pushed to his feet. After retrieving her nightie, he handed it to her before scooping her into his arms.

By process of deduction he knew which bedroom was hers. He carried her in there, laid her on the bed and pulled the covers up.

"Good night, Ryker."

"Good night, April. See you in the morning." Placing a chaste kiss on her forehead, he switched off her lamp and walked out.

Back in his own room, he braced his arms against the dresser and took several deep breaths. Close call. He hoped to God his plane could be fixed tomorrow.

* * *

April slept soundly, which surprised her. Light streamed through her bedroom window when she woke up clutching her nightie in one hand. The house was quiet so maybe Ryker was still zonked. She hoped so. He'd been through so much yesterday and then...

His hot kisses had made her forget about her tattoo. It had changed the mood, and that had been for the best. She'd learned one thing, though. He could turn her on like no other man.

She'd assigned him the hall bathroom she used to share with Leigh and she'd moved her things temporarily into her parents' master bath. On her way to shower and change, she resisted the urge to peek into Leigh's room to see if he was still asleep.

Viewed in bright morning sunshine, her encounter with him on the porch didn't seem real, although her mouth was slightly tender from his kisses. She showered quickly and dressed in jeans, t-shirt and her trusty sandals. Then she spied her dad's shaving cream on the counter. She'd provided razors but no shaving cream. She'd put that in the hall bathroom for Ryker before she went out to feed the goats and chickens.

She took the can into the bathroom he was using and discovered she was too late. He'd opened the razors and used one recently. Drops of water still clung to it.

He wasn't in the living room or the kitchen. When she went out onto the back porch, movement drew her attention to the goat pen. He was playing with the princesses. They must have been fed or they wouldn't be interested in playing games.

As he cavorted with the goats, his laughter made her smile. When he got tickled, the responsible guy who carried the world on his shoulders turned into a fun-loving kid.

She went down the steps and circled the gardens. One glance into the chicken yard told her they'd been fed, too. All the girls were busily pecking at the ground and making happy little chicken noises.

The more interesting action was in the goat pen. Ryker had a soccer ball in each hand and he'd established a rhythm of throwing them alternately to the goats, who'd butt them back to him. It was clearly a drill and pure genius for gently exercising his bum shoulder plus entertaining the goats. And him, judging from his laughter.

Then he leaped for a ball and lost his hat. The goats spied it and the race was on to see who'd snatch it up first. To her relief, Ryker won. If he hadn't grabbed it, the goats would have made short work of his lucky hat.

His attachment to it gave her a clue that he wasn't as dismissive as he used to be about such things. The Ryker she used to know would never have owned a lucky hat or suggested she use a crystal to help them make it to Kalispell.

He hadn't spotted her yet, so she watched him fool around with the goats because it made her happy. This was the side of him she loved most. When Kendra had discovered a family of skunks living under her porch, Ryker had been the one who'd insisted on trapping and relocating them. He'd been sprayed for his troubles but he'd made a joke out of it.

She'd hoped to appeal to his gentle nature when she'd tried to convince him not to enlist. She couldn't imagine how a man who couldn't kill a family of skunks would be able to take human lives. She'd believed it would scar him forever. Judging from his reaction to the fireworks, it might have.

Yet he still said he was glad he'd enlisted. She didn't get it. Which meant last night had ended the way it should have. She didn't know how to be with someone who could rescue skunks yet fire deadly missiles.

He threw the ball toward Snow White and when she butted it back, he leaped and missed.

"Point for Snow White!" Grinning, he walked over to retrieve the ball and spotted April. "Hey, there." Sure enough, he was freshly shaven.

"I forgot to give you shaving cream."

"No worries. I lathered up with soap."

"How's your shoulder?"

He rolled it. "Better. I figured a little exercise would help, too, and it does."

She gestured toward the goats. "Amused, yet?"

"I admit it. The princesses are a lot of fun. If anybody at Wild Creek Ranch liked goat milk, then goats would be a great addition. But that's not the case. The fridge is stocked with cow's milk and the freezer is full of ice cream."

"Fair enough. Do you need more time to work out or are you ready to try some of those colored eggs for breakfast?"

"I forgot to ask, are they blue when you cook them? I don't think I could deal with that."

"They look like normal eggs inside. Sometimes the yolks are a deeper yellow, almost orange, but that's about the only difference."

"Then I'm game. If you'll wait I'll walk back to the house with you. I just need a moment with my players."

"Sure." Oh, boy. He was being charming again. She couldn't hear all that he said to each of the goats but he sounded like a coach congratulating team members for their effort.

The princesses had obviously taken to him, and why not? They were athletes, too. Her dad had never played sports because he didn't believe in competition. The goats had never had a workout with him to equal this morning's drill with Ryker.

When he walked toward the gate, they followed him like groupies. April understood the feeling. He inspired that kind of adoration.

He managed to exit the pen without any goats pushing through after him. His smile faded and his expression grew tentative as he came toward her. "How are you?"

"I'm good."

"Last night was my fault. I shouldn't have—"

"Hey, no fair taking all the blame. We were both participating. Let's leave it at that."

He held her gaze. Then he gave a short nod. "All right."

"I thought we'd have veggie omelets if that works for you."

"Love 'em. Let's eat out on the back porch so we can look at the gardens, the goats and the chickens. It's peaceful."

"Okay." She wasn't so sure about the peacefulness. Now that he'd mentioned last night, her libido had perked up again. But she ought to be able to manage breakfast and the ride to the airport.

It turned out that Ryker couldn't avoid being sexy, even in the process of cooking and eating a meal. He was a big help in the kitchen, which only added to his appeal. When they'd been dating, she'd had few opportunities to notice that he knew his way around a stove.

He took charge of the country fries while she concentrated on the omelets. Or tried to.

Standing next to him at the stove while they chatted about the goats and chickens jacked up her pulse rate. All she had to do was move a little bit and her hip would brush his. If she put down her spatula and turned to him, would he ignore her or haul her into his arms?

Somehow she kept from ruining the omelets. He finished up the potatoes while she set the table and arranged the placemats on the same side so they could both enjoy the view. In the process of eating breakfast with Ryker, she learned two things that hadn't been part of their high school romance, either. He liked his coffee strong and black, and he put ketchup on his eggs.

When he poured some over his omelet, she shuddered. "That's gross."

"Don't knock it 'til you've tried it." He cut out a small section, dipped it in ketchup, and held it out on his fork. "I dare you."

She took the bite he gave her, chewed and swallowed. "Yuck."

"It's an acquired taste."

"It's an insult to the eggs those ladies produced."

"You don't know that." He sipped his coffee. "The hens might be wiggling down into their cushy nests, ready to lay an egg and thinking *damn, I hope when they cook this one up they put a little ketchup on it.*"

"You're insane." She was grateful they could joke around like they used to in the old days. If there was underlying sexual tension, she'd ignore it. She was careful not to let their knees touch under the table and he seemed to be doing the same. Only a little while longer and he'd be gone.

"You're not the first person to say I'm crazy." He glanced at her. "Coach Jamison used to tell me that all the time."

"Because it was true! You were like a freight train out there. Was our quarterback ever sacked while you were on the line?"

"Not that I can remember."

"You were the ultimate competitor."

"Says the captain of the Eagles Nest Debate Team who brought home a gazillion trophies."

"I loved those debates. Competition can be exciting if you're not a jerk about it."

He nodded. "We had a couple of football players who were jerks."

"But not you. You just wanted to perform well."

"See, that's the secret, just do your best. You were the same way. I remember you wouldn't go out with me the night before a debate because you wanted to study up on the topic."

"I couldn't stand not feeling prepared."

"That's what I mean. You're smart and you plan ahead."

"I do, which is why this trip threw me off kilter. I had my visit up here totally under control. I'd made sure my schedule was clear. I had someone from Bozeman who'd agreed to cover for me at the hospital. Then Leigh went into labor two weeks early."

He looked at her over the rim of his coffee mug. "Aren't you the one who used to tell me that things happen for a reason?"

"I might have said that." Trust him to remember, too.

"I've never known you to say something you don't believe." He sipped his coffee but kept his attention on her.

She sighed. "I believe it."

"Then why were we thrown together this weekend?"

"I'm not sure, but...possibly to make peace with each other."

He finished off his coffee and put down the mug before looking at her. "I can buy that. And have we?"

"I think we have. In a way." Some might say they'd kissed and made up. "What do you think?"

His expression was gentle. "I'd say we've made progress. I don't think we're done."

7

Ryker doubted he'd ever be done with April. She'd likely have a piece of his heart forever. But at least this supercharged episode would soon be over now that the airport was in sight.

He'd tried to call about his plane while they were still at the house, but he'd been put on hold and then they'd lost the call. Showing up in person should do the trick, though. It was just a fuel pump.

Her mom's Prius had been a big improvement over the rental car. He could wear his hat and his knees weren't up against his chest. The console formed an effective barrier that kept his arm from constantly brushing hers. He kind of missed that.

In all honesty, he'd miss her, especially after what they'd been through together. They'd see each other here and there, but nothing regular, nothing planned. He had to be okay with it and he would be once he was back home and in the swing of things.

She put on the turn signal. "You seem so sure you can get out today, but what if you can't?"

"I'll get out. Which reminds me. You may not want to take me up on it, but I'd be willing to fetch you when you're ready to come back to Eagles Nest. No charge."

She glanced at him and her beaded earrings swayed with the movement. "Thank you, but—"

"Despite what happened on the way here, you'd be safer with me than in that little tin can."

She pulled up next to the terminal. "I agree. I'll upgrade to a bigger car before I drive back. And please don't think I'm rejecting your generous offer because I'm afraid of flying in your plane."

"Are you sure?"

"Absolutely. The odds of something like that happening again are a million to one, maybe higher."

"Much higher."

She met his gaze. "It's very nice of you, but I don't want to put you to the trouble and expense."

"You never know. Somebody might want to fly up here from Eagles Nest and then I'd be in the neighborhood."

"Ryker..."

"Yeah, okay. You're right. It's better if we don't get too cozy." He reached for the door handle. "Thank you for the ride, and please thank your folks for me, too. I hope you find a replacement for the peace boxers. I took the other two pairs."

"You did?"

He grinned. "I have plans for them."

"I see. Hey, listen. I'm going to circle around while you check with the mechanics."

"That's not necessary."

"It is to me. I want to be reassured that everything's a go. Guaranteed my folks will ask.

Please come back out and tell me what they say. I'll keep circling until I see you at the curb."

"If you insist."

"I do."

"Then I'll be back shortly." He touched two fingers to the brim of his battered hat and climbed out of the car. Ten minutes later he stood by the curb and watched for the Prius. Fate sure did have a wicked sense of humor.

When April arrived, he opened the car door and climbed in. "My plane's old. They're having trouble getting the right fuel pump. They estimate tomorrow at the earliest."

She gazed at him. "I'm sorry."

"Me, too."

"If you'd rather not spend more time with my family, I could drop you off at the fair."

What a dismal prospect, kicking around a fair by himself. "I can do that."

"But you don't want to."

"Honestly, no, I don't. But I also hate the idea of interrupting what's supposed to be a family occasion. Is there a movie theater along the way? You could drop me off there."

"I'm not dropping you at the movie theater. I guess you didn't notice that you're the hero of the hour. My folks will be thrilled to have you back in their clutches."

"Um, okay. But how about you?"

"I don't plan to clutch any part of you, cowboy."

He couldn't help smiling at that. "Understood. Your folks will probably go back home tonight."

"True. Then it's settled." She put the car in gear. "We're off to see the baby."

"Before we show up there, could we stop at a store so I can buy t-shirts and boxers without peace symbols?"

"We could do that."

"And that'll give you a chance to call your folks to warn them I'm still hanging around."

"Like I said, they'll be excited."

"Do you suppose they've named the baby yet?"

"No doubt."

"She's so *tiny*. I had no concept."

"It's all about scale. I'll bet she looks bigger when I hold her than when you do. You could balance her in one hand like a soccer ball."

"Not doing that. Hey, do the goats like to play in the evening, too?"

"They might if I didn't close them in while they're eating dinner. I think you're getting attached to the princesses."

"I am. Especially Belle. She's a tricky one. You think she's not paying attention, but when I throw the ball, she's on it. Then she wags her tail because she's so proud of herself."

"Then let's do our best to make it back over there for goat playtime." She turned into the parking lot of a large retail store. "This place will have what you need."

"You don't have to go in if you want to stay here. I'll only be a minute."

"I'll go in. I might see something for the baby."

He hadn't considered that. Now that he was going back to see that little girl, he wanted to take her something.

Once April parked, the roomier Prius allowed him to get out and open April's door for her.

She smiled up at him. "It was killing you that you couldn't make it out of the little car in time, wasn't it?"

"Yep. It's not how I operate."

"Well, thank you for getting the door." She had a cute little twinkle in her brown eyes.

He was a sucker for that twinkle. She used to flirt with him in English class junior year, which was how the whole thing got started. She'd offered to help him with his homework. He'd fallen for her over verbs and participles.

Once they were inside the store, she headed off to the baby section and he promised to meet her there after he'd picked up what he needed. The store had a fair number of cowboys shopping this morning, most likely here for the rodeo that was part of the fair. He didn't recognize anybody, but he'd been gone a while.

He grabbed a package of three t-shirts in his size and another one of knit boxers. He'd put on the t-shirt when they got back to the car. The one he had on was ripe. He'd love to change out of the roomy boxers, too, but that would require stepping into the men's room after he purchased them and he didn't want to waste the time. Maybe he'd get a chance at Leigh's house.

The baby section was easy to find. Lots of pink and blue, plus cribs, strollers, baby clothes and all manner of baby equipment. He had no idea what to get that tiny girl. He spotted April at the far end of the aisle looking at jumpers and sleepwear, but that wasn't his style.

He surveyed the landscape and there they were. Bears. He'd get her a bear. But which one? She was tiny now, but she'd grow. She needed a bear that would watch over her when she was little and be a snuggle friend when she got bigger. He preferred the brown ones because they were more true to life. Kids shouldn't be thinking that bears came in pastels.

That one had a nice expression on its face. The eyes looked kind. Some eyes looked positively mean. It was about three feet tall, which seemed right to him. She wouldn't outgrow this bear. He picked it up and walked to the end of the aisle where April was still debating what to buy.

She glanced up and laughed. "That's for the baby?"

"Why not?"

"It's huge!"

"She'll grow into it."

Her gaze softened. "I suppose she will, at that. No sense it getting a puny bear, right?"

"That's what I thought."

She held up two outfits, one that looked like fake overalls and the other was covered in rainbows. "Which do you think?"

"The overalls. If your folks have anything to say about it, she'll turn into a gardener."

"You're right. They'll have her planting seedlings as soon as she can walk. They'll think this one is cute and it's a hundred-percent organic cotton, which is a bonus."

"Does that matter?"

"It's nice if you can find it, but it's not always available."

He checked the label on the bear. "Polyester. Should I put it back?"

"Absolutely not! Leigh and I had plenty of polyester stuffed animals. She'll love that bear."

"Then we're done. Did you call your parents?"

"I only talked to Mom because Dad has to work at the hospital today. But like I expected, she's sorry you have issues with your plane but she loves the idea that you'll be spending more time with us."

"Good to know. I—"

"Ryker and April! I can't believe it!" A tall cowboy hurried toward them. "It's so good to see you guys!"

Ryker searched for a name and finally came up with it. "Bob Adams! How've you been, buddy?" He shook the guy's hand.

"Never better! Racking up points for a championship buckle over at the rodeo!"

"Congratulations." Ryker clapped him on the back. "That's terrific. April, you remember Bob, right? Tight end for the Golden Eagles. Caught the touchdown pass for the division championship."

"Good to see you, Bob." April gave him a vague smile that indicated she had no idea who he was.

"Couldn't have done it without this guy." Bob grinned at him. "You mowed 'em down for me, Ryker."

"Did my best."

"So, it's obvious you two ended up together, like we all expected you would. I figured the breakup wouldn't last. Buying stuff for the little one, are you?"

"Uh, not our little one." Ryker hurried to set him straight. "These are for April's niece and we're not—"

"My mistake, my mistake. You're smart, not having kids yet. They can seriously cramp your style. I'm not even ready for that walk down the aisle, let alone a mortgage and diapers, you know what I mean?"

"Absolutely," April said. "Which is why Ryker and I aren't married. Now if you'll excuse us, we're running late for my niece's christening. Ryker, we need to go."

"Uh, yes. Yes, we do. Good luck in the arena, Bob." Ryker shook his hand again before following April down the aisle. She could move fast for a small person.

As they stood in the checkout line, he glanced at her. "Christening? Doesn't that come later? She was born yesterday."

"It was the most vital baby event I could come up with to get us out of there before things got even more complicated."

"I'm pretty sure he has the impression that we're living together."

"He might. Does it matter?"

"Guess not. I just never expected to bump into him. Got me discombobulated."

"Montana's a big state, but in some ways, it's a small state. I'm used to running into people I know." She paid for her purchase and whipped out a canvas bag from her backpack to put the onesie in. Then she gestured toward him. "Don't give him a bag, either. His stuff can go in mine, except for the bear, and we don't need a bag for that."

Ryker wasn't used to the canvas bag routine but he could see the wisdom in it. He carried both bag and bear to the car and opened her door for her before moving around to the passenger side. He put the bear on the seat and his hat on the bear. "If you don't mind waiting a minute, I want to change out of this stinky shirt before I get back in the car."

"That's fine."

He ripped open the package, pulled off his stinky shirt and put on a clean one. His soiled shirt didn't belong in the bag with a baby outfit so he rolled it up and put it on the floor mat. After moving the bear so he could sit down, he put on his hat and buckled up. "Thanks. What are you grinning about?"

"I guess you didn't notice your audience."

"What audience?"

"You gave a group of teenage girls quite a thrill by whipping off your shirt. I saw some phones come out."

Heat traveled up his neck. "I should have waited until we got to Leigh's, huh?"

"Nah." She started the car and drove out of the parking lot. "You made their day."

He sighed and leaned back against the seat. "I've been living with a bunch of guys for too long. I've forgotten how to act civilized."

"Hey, don't worry about it. You weren't showing off, just changing your shirt. They started watching you when they saw you with the bear and then the show just got better."

"Not my intention. Let's talk about something else."

"Okay." She was still smiling when she glanced over at him. "That's a really big bear. It's the size of a preschooler."

"Someday she'll be a preschooler and they can be friends. When she's bigger, she can be like the older sister. It'll work."

"I know it will. I'm just teasing you. This takes me back to the time you won a bear for me at the carnival that came through town."

"Oh, yeah, I remember that carnival, all right. What crooks, gluing the milk bottles together so nobody could knock 'em over."

"I never laughed so much in my life. I don't think they anticipated someone who could throw a baseball that hard. Goodbye, milk bottles."

"I don't suppose you still have that bear."

Her voice was sad. "No, I don't suppose I do."

"Did you get rid of everything I gave you?"

She hesitated. "Almost."

Uh-oh. "Promise me you didn't keep that sappy poem." When she didn't answer, he groaned.

"I can barely remember it but I'm sure it was stupid. If you care about me at all, you'll go home and burn it."

"I kept it because you put blood, sweat and tears into writing it. I asked you for a poem and you accepted the challenge even though it wasn't your strong suit. It was the best thing you ever gave me."

"If that's true, everything else must have been crappy."

"No, you gave me some really nice things, but they're all gone. The poem was something you couldn't buy or win for me. You had to dig it out of your soul."

"Oh, jeez. That says it all. Have pity on me, April. I was an eighteen-year-old guy in love for the first time. No telling what kind of sentimental garbage I spewed out."

"I can recite it."

"Please don't. I might puke."

"You won't, but I'll hold off because we're almost at Leigh's house. I might recite it to you this evening if I get a chance."

"I'll be busy playing with the goats."

"I can work around that."

He didn't doubt it. Her brand of smarts included ingenuity. But he'd rather be court-martialed than listen to her recite that poem. Once she was back in Eagles Nest, he'd convince her to destroy the physical copy. He didn't want it floating around, although if she'd memorized it...and why had she done that?

He was so distracted when she parked the car in Leigh's driveway that he forgot to leap out and open her door. He also had to deal with the bear and didn't want to accidentally drop it in the dirt. He gave her the overalls from the bag and carried the bear. So much had happened since the first time he walked up the steps to this porch.

"For the record, I'm jealous that you went for the bear and I got an outfit."

"If you want to switch presents, I'll give her the overalls."

"You'd let me hand over the bear as if I'm the one who chose it?"

"Why not? I don't care who gets the credit. I just think she needs a big cuddly bear."

"You're such a good guy."

"I wouldn't say that."

"I would. You thought of the bear and you should take it to her. Or take it to Leigh. She'll fall in love with it, too. It has a good expression on its face."

He smiled. "I know."

8

April walked into the living room with Ryker behind her. "We're here!"

"We're in the kitchen!" her mom called out. "Leigh's feeding Pax."

Ryker took off his hat and looked at April. "They have a dog?"

She put a finger to her lips and hustled him back toward the front door. Then she motioned for him to lean down so she could talk quietly. "I think that's her name."

"Whose name?"

"The baby."

His eyes widened. "You're kidding."

She shook her head.

"Packs?" He frowned. "Like in six-packs? What kind of a name is—"

"No, Pax with an X. It means peace in Latin."

He stared at her in confusion. "I still think it's a dog."

"They don't have a dog. Let's go in before they start wondering what we're whispering about."

She raised her voice. "We brought presents but I'm afraid they're not wrapped."

Her mom laughed. "Pax won't care, will she, Leigh?"

"Nope, and wrapping's a waste of resources, anyway."

Ryker left his hat on the mantel in the living room and April led the way into the kitchen. John was at the stove cooking breakfast, his blond hair in a short ponytail, and her mom was sitting at the kitchen table folding laundry with Leigh next to her nursing Pax. For Ryker's sake, April was relieved that Leigh had thrown a baby blanket over her exposed breast and the newborn. He might not be up to a full reveal.

Leigh smiled when she saw the teddy bear. "Ryker, that's *adorable*. Thank you."

John turned from the stove and gave Ryker a thumbs-up. "Awesome. She'll love that."

"She will." April's mom beamed at him. "Every baby needs a teddy bear."

Ryker seemed pleased with the reception. "I know it's a little big."

"No worries," Leigh said. "She'll grow into it."

"That's what I thought." Ryker glanced around the room. "Where is she?"

April ducked her head to hide a grin.

"Under here." Leigh moved a bottom section of the blanket to reveal a tiny foot.

"Oh." He blushed. "Well, um, where should I put the bear?"

April's mom waved a hand toward a corner of the kitchen. "How about in the high chair for now? Pax won't be using it for a while, so the bear will look cute holding her place."

"Sounds good." Ryker gently worked the stuffed animal's body down into the vintage wooden high chair.

April started to tell him he could move the tray but he already had the bear wedged in so there was no point. He hadn't been kidding when he told her he didn't know anything about babies. Now that the bear had been properly admired, April held up the overalls. "I couldn't resist."

"Oh, my!" Her mom held out her hand. "Let me see that. Would it fit her now, do you think?"

Leigh chuckled. "We could make it fit if Auntie April wants a photo op. Well done, sis. Very sweet."

"And it's made with organic cotton," Ryker said.

"Is it?" Her mom checked the label. "So it is. That's great."

"The bear's not, though. Sorry about that."

Her mom gave him another big smile. "Plush animals usually aren't and that's fine. It's a gorgeous bear."

"Oatmeal's almost ready." John tapped the spoon on the side of the pot. "Who wants some?"

"I do." Leigh rose carefully from her chair. "But I need to change Pax and put her down for a nap. Maybe Auntie April would like to assist."

"You bet." April went over to steady her sister.

"Thanks. I'm not as nimble today as I normally am."

"You're doing great." April glanced back at John. "Ryker and I already had breakfast, but I'd love some coffee when Leigh and I get back."

"I had breakfast," Ryker said, "but the oatmeal smells great. If there's enough, I'll have a little."

"There's plenty," John said.

"And he makes great oatmeal," Leigh called over her shoulder as April guided her and the baby back to the master bedroom.

"How are you feeling?" April edged sideways through the doorway while keeping a hand on Leigh.

"Sore as hell. But you can let go of me. And close the door, please."

"Do you need to change clothes?"

"No, I want to hear about last night! I was so out of it I didn't realize that by asking Mom and Dad to stay we were leaving you alone in the house with your ex-boyfriend!"

"Shh."

"They can't hear us. These doors are solid."

"I'm worried you'll wake Pax."

"Not likely." She removed the blanket and laid the sleeping baby on a changing table. "She doesn't sleep for long, but when she's out, she's out."

"Oh, Leigh, she's beautiful." April gazed at the tiny girl with the fuzzy hair and the perfect little rosebud mouth. The tie-dyed onesie in blues and greens made her look like a nymph from the forest. "You did that tie-dye job, didn't you?"

"Mom helped. We bought plain white and created our own designs. I'll save them for you if you think some day you might—"

"I have my doubts."

"What about Mr. Pilot Hero out there?" She unsnapped the crotch of the onesie. "So you and Ryker—is there still a spark? Because I'm sensing a vibe between you two."

"There's still a spark. I mean, look at the guy."

"I did when he walked in with that teddy bear. Damn, woman. Seems like you should fan that flame."

"That part would be easy. Listen, can I help with anything? I'm just standing here."

"I didn't really ask you in here to help." Leigh expertly cleaned the baby and put on a fresh diaper. "I wanted the scoop. Are you two going to get jiggy or what?"

"I think it's a bad idea."

"But you want to."

"I'm only human and he's..."

"A walking fantasy?"

"Yes, yes he is. Complete with a sexy armband."

"I noticed that, too."

"Oh, and incidentally, while he was serving his country, he managed to get himself shot."

"He told you?"

"No. I saw the scarring."

"And where was this scarring, pray tell?" Leigh snapped the onesie back in place.

"On his back near his scapula. If the bullet had hit his spine he could be paralyzed. If it had hit his heart he could be dead."

"Instead he's alive and looking like God's gift. How did you happen to see this scar?"

"I gave him a massage."

"Aha. The plot thickens." Leigh picked up the baby and laid her in a wooden cradle. "And then what?"

"He went off to take a shower and I went to bed."

"That's it? Talk about anticlimactic. Literally."

"There was one more thing. The fireworks woke him and made him nervous. It was too much like gunfire."

"I've always said that." Leigh gazed at her. "Did you comfort him?"

"In a way."

"Mm."

"But then he saw my dove tattoo."

"I can see what this comforting must have involved."

"We didn't really do anything, if that's what you're thinking. The dove tattoo put an end to it."

Leigh's eyebrow's rose. "It came to life and told him to back off?"

"No." April laughed. "Honestly, Leigh."

"I was just trying to get you to lighten up. Hang on a minute." She walked into the master bath and came back holding something. "Put out your hand."

"What have you got?"

"Put out your hand and you'll find out."

April sighed and did as she was told.

Leigh laid several foil packets in her palm. "Take these. They're from a box John bought and never opened because we decided to start a family."

"I don't need them." She tried to give them back but Leigh put both hands behind her back. "Okay, then I'll leave them on your bathroom counter." She started in that direction.

"I'd advise against it."

"Why?"

"Because I've asked Mom and Dad to stay here again tonight. It's a huge help when Pax is getting up every two hours and John and I need more rest."

"You're making that up because you want me to get horizontal with Ryker."

"I'm not making that up. I desperately want them both here, but I also think you and Ryker need to talk, and you won't be able to have a sensible discussion until you wear each other out in bed."

Now there was a riveting concept.

"See? You're thinking about it. Think about it some more and you'll know I'm right. Put the condoms in your pocket. Nobody has to know you have them unless you want them to."

"That's true." She put two in each front pocket. "But now I know they're there. I won't be able to forget it."

Leigh came over and grasped her arms. "Sis, you're gonna be alone with that cowboy again tonight and he's a walking, talking fantasy. I think it's wise to be prepared."

* * *

When April came back with Leigh, the two of them looked like they'd been up to something. Ryker couldn't imagine what. They'd only gone in there to change the baby and put her to bed, but he couldn't shake the suspicion that more had taken place. Like girl talk. About him.

While they'd been gone, he'd helped set the table, toasted the bread and made a pot of decaf for Leigh who couldn't drink the real stuff. Eileen had brought over an extra coffee maker from her house so that Leigh could always have decaf brewing and John could have his leaded version. Ryker used to think vegetarians drank mostly herbal tea, but these two were hard-core coffee fanatics.

Everyone gathered around the kitchen table, and April was the only one who didn't want a bowl of oatmeal. Ryker was thrilled to have it. He loved the stuff, just like his dad used to. Maybe that was why he enjoyed it so much. Recently he'd found out how healthy it was.

Leigh and John liked it topped with organic dried cranberries, and he'd decided that was an excellent combo. He was nearly finished with one bowl and debating a second when John asked the question he'd been dreading.

"Hey, Ryker, what do you think of the name Pax?"

"It's different, all right."

"Different, yet universal." John glanced fondly at his wife. "Leigh and I love the sentiment behind the name, and it's somewhat gender neutral."

"You could say that." Ryker struggled to be diplomatic. Pax sounded like a guy name to him, but he'd keep his mouth shut.

He liked Leigh and John. Even if he hated the name they'd chosen, which he did, they were the ones who should decide. It wasn't as if they had to take a poll and use the one with the most votes. They thought Pax was a nifty name and he wouldn't rain on their parade for anything.

"I love it, too," April said. "You might have trouble finding that name on a keychain, but we're moving into an era of keyless locks, anyway."

Her mom shook her head. "Keychains aren't the fun accessories they used to be. I would let you girls play with my keys when we were out somewhere and you got fussy. Now I wouldn't dare let a child have them. They'd set off my car alarm for sure."

"I've seen fake keys for little kids," John said. "Wooden ones, too, instead of plastic."

"I've seen those," April's mom said. "I can't believe babies would go for them. They want the taste of metal and whatever other jingly stuff you have on there. Fake keys don't make the same kind of noise."

"I think kids know they aren't real, that they don't really do anything." Ryker didn't know much about babies but this was a topic he was passionate about. "I always wanted to play with whatever the adults had. When I was around seven I took apart my mom's hair dryer."

April laughed. "I never heard about that."

"I wasn't exactly proud of doing it. Nearly electrocuted myself. Messed it up so bad she had to get a new one. But I had this idea that a hair dryer was like a mini jet engine. I wanted to get the handle off so I could attach the business end to my toy plane. I figured if I hooked a bunch of extension cords together I could fly it around the room."

John nodded. "I can see a kid thinking that might work. So did you always want to fly?"

"Ever since I can remember. I have a vivid memory of sitting with my dad in the living room when I was four or five watching *Top Gun* on TV. He loved that movie."

"Loved?" John frowned. "Then he's..."

"He died at twenty-four. Brain aneurism."

Eileen reached over and squeezed his arm. "That was such a tragedy for your mom. I always admired her for raising the five of you by herself."

"She's an incredible woman."

"I remember thinking that when we lived there. Tell her hello for me, will you?"

"Definitely. That reminds me I need to call her and say I won't be home today. If you'll excuse me, I'll go out back and make that call." Then he glanced at the dirty dishes on the table. "On second thought, I'll do it after we clean up."

"Go ahead," Eileen said. "John, you cooked, so you go relax. The ladies will take care of this."

John stood and stretched. "Thank you, but I'm not in the mood to relax. Think I'll tackle that woodpile."

"You heat the house with wood?" Ryker was intrigued.

"Not exactly, but Leigh's crazy about a wood fire."

"Then after I finish my call I'll help you." His shoulder was tightening up again and a little bit of work with an axe might be just the ticket. After retrieving his hat from the living room, he followed John through the screened back porch and out into the yard. "This screened porch concept is nice. We don't have that at the ranch."

"Leigh was used to having one when she lived with her folks, so we made sure the house we bought had one, too. It'll be great for Pax next summer." He paused. "Eileen told me you made it here on one engine."

"Yeah, it was a little tense."

"No kidding. Probably not the worst thing you've faced, but still."

"Right. I'd rather not have to do it again."

John shoved his hands in the pockets of his loose cotton pants. "What type of jet did you fly over there?"

"F-15 Eagle."

"Now there's a classic fighter. Hasn't it been in service for like thirty years?"

"As a matter of fact." Ryker gazed at him. "Are you into planes?"

"I'm into jets. If my eyesight had been better, I'd be in the military flying instead of working as a nurse. But when I found out I couldn't be a pilot because of my eyes, I decided not to enlist."

"Does Leigh know all that?"

"She does, but we decided it wasn't something we had to tell her folks. My family lives in Idaho and that's where I was when I tried to enlist, so there's no reason for her parents to know. I might have made a lousy soldier, anyway, but the military was the only way I'd ever get to fly jets so I was ready to go for it."

"Sorry it didn't work out."

"I'm not."

"Well, yeah. If your eyes had been better, you wouldn't have met Leigh and you wouldn't have Pax."

"Exactly. When I look at those two, I'm grateful for my bad eyes. But tell me the truth. Was it awesome?"

Ryker smiled. "It was awesome. Except for the part where somebody starts shooting at you."

"Scary?"

"You don't believe it will be, not when you're that age, anyway. You train for it and you're hot to get up there, chomping at the bit to engage the enemy. Then the day comes, your first dogfight. And it occurs to you that holy crap, this isn't a video game. Someone's trying to kill your ass. It's a sobering moment."

"I guess it would be. So why didn't you get out after your first tour?"

He hesitated. "It cost me a lot to go in."

"So I hear. Leigh told me a little. She was only fourteen at the time, but she had a fair idea of how bad that breakup was, at least from April's perspective."

"I'm sure it was hard on her." Ryker pictured her tattoo. "And it may sound stupid, but after what I gave up to go in, I had to stay long enough that I could feel I'd made a substantial contribution, that it was worth the sacrifice."

"It doesn't sound stupid to me, but I'm not April. Is there any chance you two can work it out?"

"I can't speak for her, but the stakes are too high for me. I never want to feel that kind of misery again."

"I understand." John sighed. "Anyway, I should let you make your call. I'll be over at the woodpile splitting logs. Come on by when you're finished."

"I'll be there in a few."

John started toward the large pile of wood stacked on the far side of the property, but then he turned back. "I just wanted you to know you're not the only one in this group who thinks jets are cool."

"I appreciate that." He pulled out his phone and dialed his mom.

This time when she answered a horse whinnied in the background. "You just caught me. Another ten minutes and some folks will be here to take a trail ride. Zane and I just finished saddling everybody."

"It's a short ride, I hope."

"Yes, it's a short one. After all this time, I'm not going to push my luck."

"Good. Listen, I won't be home today, either. The part wasn't available so it'll be tomorrow, looks like."

"Okay. Sorry you're running up a hotel bill, though."

"As it turns out, I'm not. I'm staying with April's folks."

"Oh, really?"

"And Eileen said to tell you hello."

"Tell her the same for me. What an interesting development. Can't wait to hear all about it. Oh, and Ellie Mae Stockton called. She's on the committee for the Labor Day Parade and she wants you to wear your uniform and maybe give a speech after the parade."

He groaned. "What did you tell her?"

"That it's up to you. Hey, gotta go. See you soon. Love you." She disconnected the call.

A speech. Hell, no. But his family had always ridden in the parade so he'd figured on doing it with them since he'd be home and available. He hadn't planned to wear his uniform, though. Good thing he didn't have to decide right this minute because he was torn between his patriotic duty and his reluctance to draw attention to himself.

Sending a quick text to Joe, he tucked his phone away and crossed the grassy backyard to the woodpile where John was splitting logs. He was almost there when John swore and dropped the axe.

He hurried forward. "You okay?"

"No. Sliced my damn hand." He started for the house. "Just look at this! I'll probably need stitches."

Ryker glanced at John's bloody hand. It was the last thing he saw before darkness closed in.

9

April was at the sink washing dishes and laughing at the raunchy joke Leigh had just told when John burst into the kitchen trailing blood.

"Ryker's down!" Then he grabbed the towel Leigh was using and wrapped his hand.

"John, what—"

"I'm fine. Stay with the baby!" Then he dashed back out the door.

April ran after him, anxiety blurring her vision. Ryker was motionless, lying face down by the woodpile, his hat nearby. She'd never seen this happen but she'd heard about it from his brothers. They'd thought she needed to be prepared, just in case. Ryker had been upset that his brothers had revealed a supposed weakness to his girlfriend.

Thank goodness they'd told her or she'd be even more panicked. Even knowing the likely cause, she could barely breathe and her heart pounded like a runaway horse.

"I would have...flipped him...to his back," John gasped out. "But I would have bled on him."

"That would only make it worse." She dropped down by his side. "I'm guessing it was the blood that made him faint."

"Then I need to stay out of his field of vision."

"Good idea."

"I'm here." Her mom arrived out of breath and sank to her knees in the grass. "I grabbed my phone. In case we have to call 911."

"We shouldn't have to, unless he hit his head or dislocated something. He faints at the sight of blood."

"Poor guy! I'll bet he hates that."

"I'm sure he does."

Her mom glanced up at John. "You're the nurse in this group. Tell us what to do."

"Once you roll him to his back, elevate his feet. I'll drag a couple of logs closer and you can use those."

"That should work." April leaned over Ryker's broad back and got a grip on his side. "Mom, grab his left leg."

"Got it. John, how's your hand?"

"I'm applying pressure to the wound. I'll be okay for now."

April glanced at her mom. "On the count of three. One, two, *three.*" With a loud groan, she managed to pull him halfway so he was lying on his side.

Her mom was puffing from the effort of dragging his lower body somewhat into alignment with his torso. "It's like trying to maneuver a two-hundred-and-thirty-pound rag doll."

"Check for contusions now that you have access to his face," John said. "If he hit his head then we have another set of problems."

"I don't see any sign of that." April gently brushed away some grass stuck to his cheek.

"Look under his hairline."

She combed her fingers through his short hair and felt for any bumps or bleeding. Tender emotions tugged at her heart. "Nothing."

"Then let's get him onto his back."

She glanced up at John. "We should probably lower him slowly so he doesn't crash to the ground, right?"

"Just the opposite. We need to wake him up, and letting him fall to his back might jostle him enough to bring him out of it."

"All right, then." She took a deep breath. "Mom, let's move to the other side and push." She waited until they were both in position with their hands braced against him. "Shove hard."

He toppled over and lay there sprawled in the grass looking incredibly vulnerable. He'd be so embarrassed when he came to. She hated that for him.

"Lift his legs," John said. "I'll push these logs underneath."

With April on one leg and her mom on the other, they managed it.

"Now one of you loosen his clothing."

April backed away. "He's all yours, Mom."

"That makes no sense. You're the one who...oh, all right." Kneeling, she unfastened the button on his Wranglers. "John, tell me that's good enough."

"I think it's good enough. He just opened his eyes. April, make sure he doesn't get up too fast. He could be dizzy."

April grabbed his hat before crouching beside him and smoothing her hand over his cheek. "Ryker?"

He blinked and stared up at her. "What happened?"

"You passed out."

"Fuck." Then he squeezed his eyes shut. "Who's out here with you?"

"My mom and John."

He groaned. "Excuse my language, Eileen."

"You're excused, Ryker."

"Thanks." He started to sit up.

April placed a hand on his chest. "Easy does it, cowboy. You might be dizzy."

"Did you say John's here?" He sank back to the ground and closed his eyes. "I'm not going to look at you, John, but how's the hand, buddy?"

"It'll be fine."

"But you said you needed stitches." Ryker tried to get up again and April restrained him.

"I might need a few," John said. "I'll go to the ER in a bit. Right now you should stay horizontal and let your body recover."

"That's not my style. I'm…hey, how come my jeans are unbuttoned?"

"My mom did that after John said we should loosen your clothing."

"Huh." He refastened the button. "Okay, April, don't try to hold me down, sweetheart. I'm getting up and that's final."

Sweetheart? She shot a glance at her mom. "He's not quite himself," she mumbled.

Her mom just smiled.

Ryker unfolding from the ground was like a large inflatable yard ornament being filled with air. He rose to one knee. Then he staggered up until he stood, swaying and breathing hard. At last he inhaled and threw back his shoulders. "That's better." He glanced at the ground. "Where's my hat?"

"Right here." She handed it to him.

"Thank you." He put it on and adjusted the brim. "That's that. Now John needs to get to the ER."

"I'll take him." April's mom glanced at her. "Are the keys in your backpack?"

"Front zipper pocket."

She nodded. "Take care of Ryker while we're gone."

"Fruit juice," Holding his hand behind his back, John eased away from his position behind Ryker. "The sugar will give him a boost. Keep him hydrated."

"I'm *fine*."

April's mom walked over and patted his arm. "I know you are, sweetie, but you need some TLC. April, the diffuser's on the kitchen counter and it needs water. I'll bet some lavender oil mist would be good."

"I'll do that. Before you leave you should make sure you reassure Leigh. I'm surprised she didn't scoop up Pax and come running out here because she was worried about John."

"Me, too," John said. "Oh, look. Here she comes."

Clutching a blanket-wrapped Pax to her chest, Leigh hurried toward them. "I gave up on anybody coming inside to inform me. I see Ryker's standing. John, why are you hiding your hand?"

"Just didn't want to freak you out."

"Like you would. I grew up with this stuff. Speaking of that, do you need to go to the ER?"

"Probably should get a few stitches. Your mom's taking me. If we ask nicely, we might get your dad to do it."

"You should. He's an artist."

Ryker turned pale and swayed.

April grabbed his arm but it was a token gesture. If he went down, they'd both hit the ground.

Her mom motioned to John. "Let's move it, Jonathan."

John kept his attention on Ryker as he edged around him, his hand tucked behind his back. "Get some fruit juice into him, April."

"I will."

"I'm fine." Ryker didn't sound fine.

April sent John a confident smile. Her sweet brother-in-law needed to take off so Ryker could forget about blood and stitches. "Don't worry. Leigh and I will manage everything here."

"Definitely." Leigh jiggled Pax as the baby began to whimper. "Make them give you a lollipop, John."

"Oh, yeah. My heart's set on grape." By walking sideways, he kept his hand hidden as he passed Ryker. Then he held it in front of him as he lengthened his stride to catch up with April's mom, who was already on the porch.

Leigh gazed after him. "Does it seem like John's acting a little weird?"

"It's not John." Ryker's voice was laced with humiliation. "It's me. Blood makes me pass out. He's trying to make sure I don't do it again."

"Oh, wow. Bummer." She jiggled Pax a little more vigorously as the baby's whimpering became actual crying. "Sorry. She's hungry."

"Go feed her," April said. "We'll be up at the house shortly."

"If you're sure you'll be okay."

"I'm sure."

Once Leigh was back on the porch, Ryker let out a breath. "I feel like a damned pansy-ass."

"Right. The same pansy-ass who didn't flinch when his plane lost an engine."

"That's different."

"Ryker, it's a phobia. We all have them. I used to be afraid of spiders."

"Yeah, but you didn't pass out when you saw them."

"No, I got hysterical. Yelled like my hair was on fire. Would you rather have that reaction to your phobia? Screaming like a little girl?"

A hint of a smile was like a break in the clouds. "When you put it that way, passing out is more manly, but I still hate it. Are you saying you're not afraid of spiders anymore?"

"That's right."

"How'd you get over it?"

"Hypnotherapy."

"Oh. Sorry, but that wouldn't work for me."

"Why not?"

His jaw tightened. "I don't like the idea of somebody taking over my brain."

"That's not what happens. They help you access your subconscious so you can drill down and change the behavior from the inside out."

"No, thanks. I appreciate the suggestion, but that's not for me."

"All right, then. Let me know if you ever change your mind." Many times in the past she'd wanted to shake him, and this was another one. It would be a pointless exercise because there was no shaking a guy built like Ryker. Except maybe right now, when he wasn't so rock steady. "Do you feel like walking up to the house?"

"Sure. But I don't want you to fuss over me once we get there. I'm not big on fruit juice and lavender's liable to remind me of...you know. In fact, maybe instead of going up to the house, I'll head on back to the woodpile and split some logs for John."

She stared at him. "You're kidding me, right?"

"With his injury he's not going to be getting to it any time soon, and those logs are too big for Leigh to handle. John wants to provide a wood fire for her and that's important. Families gather around a fireplace and they're a family, now."

"Then my dad can come over and split it for them. Or one of their friends from the hospital can help out. You just took a header into the dirt. John recommended fruit juice and rest, so that's what you need to do."

He tugged the brim of his battered straw hat lower so it shaded his eyes. "I'm no good at that routine, April. I'm not the sort of guy who enjoys kicking back in a recliner and pushing buttons on the remote. I have to be doing something."

"Then we'll play cards."

He shook his head. "I'm gonna go chop wood."

"You're unbelievable." Her patience gave out. "Less than thirty minutes ago, you were out *cold*. Mom and I struggled to turn you over because you were lying there like you were dead! And now you're planning to pick up an axe and split some logs? What's wrong with you?"

"I'm grateful that you and your mom did me that kindness. I recover fast, though, and I want to do a favor for John and Leigh by stockpiling some wood for their fireplace."

She threw up her hands. "Then go ahead! But be damned careful with that axe, because if you draw blood and pass out again, we're running out of people strong enough to haul your sorry ass around!" Whirling away, she stomped back to the house swearing under her breath. Stubborn cowboy. She was still cursing when she walked into the kitchen.

Leigh sat at the kitchen table with Pax nursing under a blanket. "Where's Ryker?"

"Don't ask."

"Is he okay?"

"No, he's gone completely bonkers."

"And you're saying this because..."

"Listen carefully. Do you hear something going on in your backyard?"

Her mouth dropped open. "He's splitting logs?"

"Yes, he is."

"What if he cuts himself?"

April shrugged. "I really don't know. Or care."

"Liar. If you didn't care you wouldn't be so upset with him."

"But why is he acting like this?"

"Come on. You know why. He wants to reestablish his manly image after a humiliating experience. He can't do that drinking fruit juice and being coddled."

"But he's taking a dumb risk exerting himself so soon after passing out. What if he hurts himself out there?"

Leigh regarded her quietly. "Then I guess we'll deal with it as best we can. But I don't think you can put limits on a man like Ryker. He seems to enjoy testing himself."

"Don't I know it." She sank down on a chair across from her sister. "He's the kind of guy who'd die to save a stranger. I'm aware of his disregard for his own safety."

"Yes, but are you still hoping he'll change?"

"That would be stupid. He won't."

"Guys can make us stupid, sis."

She gazed at Leigh. "How did you get so smart?"

"Easy." She smiled. "I've been watching you."

10

"Break time!"

Ryker lowered the axe and glanced toward the house. April's dad approached carrying two open bottles of beer, moisture condensing on the glass. And man, was he parched. "Hey, Kevin. Thought you were on duty today."

"I was until three. I followed Eileen and John home. Thought you could use a cool one."

"Sure can. Thanks." He wiped his hand on his jeans and took the bottle. "Guess you heard about me passing out."

"Eileen and John filled me in." He tapped his bottle against Ryker's. "Here's to surviving in this crazy world."

"I'll drink to that." He took several swallows.

"Eileen and John wouldn't let me bring you the beer unless I promised I'd get you to drink this, too." He reached in his back pocket and pulled out a waxed carton. "It's coconut milk."

"I've had that before, except I drank it from a coconut with a hole drilled into it."

"How'd you like it?"

"Not too bad."

"This won't be as good as fresh from the coconut, but if you'll agree to swig it down then I won't get in trouble."

Ryker grinned. "Great sales pitch you have there." He set his beer on the chopping block and took the carton. After opening it, he drank half without stopping.

"Whoa, whoa. I didn't mean you had to chugalug it."

"The faster I drink it, the sooner I can go back to the beer." He polished off the other half.

Kevin stroked his short beard. "You're not much of a middle-of-the-road guy, are you?"

"Never appealed to me. Either I'm all in or I don't care to do it at all." He crushed the carton in his fist. "I'll bet you recycle these puppies."

"Ryker, we recycle *everything*. No, wait, that's wrong. We recycle everything we can't reuse. But there's no reusing that wax carton. At least not on our end. I've seen fireplace logs made from them, though." He gestured to the stack of firewood. "Let's have a seat."

Setting the crushed carton on the chopping block and retrieving his beer, Ryker joined him. "I'm surprised Leigh and John aren't burning that kind of log instead of wood."

"Sometimes they do. But Leigh likes the aesthetics of a fire made with real wood. Me, too. They'll appreciate you splitting all those logs."

"No problem. I'm grateful for the hospitality everyone's shown me, especially considering..."

"The way I heard it, she broke up with you."

"But you must have agreed with her reasons."

"Don't be too sure."

Ryker gazed at him. "Meaning?"

"Don't get me wrong. I'm behind my daughter a hundred percent no matter what she decides. I'll go to the mat for her because that's what dads do. But...I believe in personal autonomy. You followed your conscience. That's the highest calling there is."

As Kevin's words sank in, Ryker's throat tightened. "Thank you." He cleared his throat. "April objected to me going, as you know. But my family did, too, especially my mom."

"It's easier for me to be supportive of your choice. I like and respect you, but you're not my son. April had planned to spend the rest of her life with you. Your family and April are more invested in your survival than I am. I wouldn't judge them too harshly."

"But serving my country was important to me."

"And keeping you alive was important to them."

"Well, sure, but—"

"Nobody wants the person they love to become a dead hero, even if the person involved is willing to make that sacrifice."

"Isn't that kind of selfish, though?"

"Put the shoe on the other foot. What if April had a burning desire to work in some area of the world where her skills were desperately needed, but at any time she could be kidnapped by thugs who raped and tortured women?"

His gut tightened. "I wouldn't like it."

"Would you try to convince her not to go?"

"Possibly." Probably.

"And what if she went anyway? How would you react?"

He grimaced. "You ask hard questions, Kevin."

"That's my job." He took another swallow of his beer. "But enough philosophy. As you probably noticed, the eating schedule got wonky today, so everyone decided on an early dinner. It should be about ready. I don't know about you, but I could eat."

Ryker stood and picked up the crushed carton. "Lead the way. And before I forget to say it, the goats and chickens are a hoot. Goats wouldn't make sense at the ranch but chickens are a real possibility."

Kevin leaped on that topic and kept up an animated discussion about chicken coops and enclosures until they reached the back porch where April was setting the table.

She glanced up when they came through the screen door. "You made it."

Ryker wasn't exactly sure how to interpret that so he tipped his hat in her direction. "Yes, ma'am." He held out the crushed wax carton. "Where does this go?"

"There's a recycling bin on the far corner of the porch."

Eileen called from the kitchen. "If anybody out there's available to help drain the noodles, I could use a hand."

"On my way." Kevin hurried into the kitchen, leaving Ryker alone with April.

He decided an apology was in order, especially after Kevin's insights. "Sorry if I was a jerk a while ago."

She finished putting out the silverware and gazed at him. "Were you?"

"You were trying to keep me from hurting myself. I wasn't particularly cooperative."

"That's for sure." She hesitated. "Are you okay?"

"Yes, although in retrospect I should have come in for water."

"Why didn't you?"

He gazed at her. "I didn't want another lecture."

She heaved a sigh. "I was only—"

"I know. It's just that I...well, anyway. Now's not the time to talk about it."

"Looks like we'll have plenty of chances to talk later."

"We will?"

"My folks are staying here again tonight."

His heart rate shot up. "They are?"

"Leigh had wanted them to, anyway, but now that John's right hand is bandaged, he's not much use with the baby, so Leigh really needs the help."

He scrambled for a response, any response. "Wouldn't she need your help, too?"

"I asked. She was sweet about it, but the truth is that Mom knows more about babies than I do and Dad's a nurse and I'm not. I'd only be in the way."

He swallowed. "Okay, then."

"I thought you'd like to know in advance."

"Appreciate it. I'll just go toss this carton in the recycling." After he did, he stood by the bin for a second, eyes squeezed shut. Crap.

For the next hour, he made conversation with her family. He ate a meatless spaghetti dish that might have been the best he'd ever had. He helped clean up after the meal. Mostly, though, he avoided looking at April, because every time he did, he started to sweat.

They'd be alone in the house. All night. She'd be lying in her bed, in that short nightie he'd stripped off, the nightie that covered her dove tattoo. The tattoo had been enough to ruin the mood before, but he was over that, now. In fact, he wanted to see it again. In the light.

His brain told him to forget about her but his body craved that connection. Still. Despite the pain she'd caused him, despite the long separation, despite his vow to have nothing more to do with her. His sense of preservation went AWOL when she was within kissing distance. Once he left town, he'd be able to listen to his brain, but this golden opportunity had reduced his IQ to zero.

How the hell was he supposed to get through another night alone with her? Only one thing had the power to keep his lust in check. He had no condoms handy. He'd look upon that as a blessing.

* * *

The slight crinkle of the condoms in April's pockets had bedeviled her ever since Leigh had insisted she take them. She'd never found a convenient time to either return them to Leigh's bathroom or tuck them in her backpack. Worse yet, she couldn't decide which of those roads to take.

They crinkled again when she climbed behind the wheel of the Prius for the drive back to her folks' house. She dared any woman with condoms in her pocket and Ryker in the passenger seat not to think about sex. He filled her peripheral vision—straw hat tugged low, a shadow of a beard, his massive chest stretching his cotton t-shirt. Just listening to him breathe dampened her panties.

He cleared his throat. "I have a plan."

"For what?"

"Being alone in the house."

Oh, this should be good. "What's that?"

"First off, when we get there, I'll feed the goats and the chickens and tuck them in."

"What am I supposed to do?" Take a bubble bath and put on a negligee?

"Whatever you want except help me. The less time we spend together, the better."

"So your plan is total avoidance."

"Pretty much."

"Then I guess you don't want to talk about anything, either." His plan didn't have a snowball's chance in hell, but she was interested in hearing his reasons for thinking they needed one.

"Not tonight."

"In the morning, then?" She braked at a red light.

"Not then, either."

"Well, I'm confused." She glanced over at him. "This morning you seemed to think we weren't finished with the process of making peace with each other. How can we do that if we don't talk about it?"

"I don't know."

"It's obvious that we still have issues." She accelerated as the light changed. "Otherwise we wouldn't have had that blowup over whether you needed rest after you passed out."

"And maybe we always will have issues. That's likely, isn't it? We see the world differently."

"I'm sure we do. But I'll bet we can agree on one thing."

"What's that?"

"We turn each other on."

He blew out a breath. "Which is exactly why I'm proposing that we stay out of each other's way!"

"That's one solution."

"It's the one I vote for."

She allowed the silence to lengthen between them.

"I mean, isn't that what we decided last night?" He sounded a little desperate.

She pulled the car into the drive of her parents' house. "Guess so." After shutting off the motor, she turned to gaze at him. "But last night we didn't think we'd be dealing with this situation again."

"Nothing's changed. It's still a bad idea." The heat in his blue eyes said something very different.

"All right, but I don't picture myself running for my bedroom and hiding there the rest of the evening."

"You don't have to. I'll come in after feeding and go straight to mine."

She shrugged. "If that's what you want."

"Hell, April, you know that's not what I *want*. But it's the smart decision."

"Okay." She opened her door and got out. He didn't immediately follow her, so maybe he was dealing with an inconvenient reaction to their conversation.

After unlocking the front door, she glanced back at him. "I'm having a beer. Want me to get you one?"

"No, thanks."

"Suit yourself." She left the door open and dropped her backpack on the sofa on her way through the fuchsia and purple living room. The colors resonated with her tonight. She was in a fuchsia and purple mood as she headed into the kitchen and grabbed a bottle of beer out of the refrigerator.

The front door closed. "Want me to lock it?" he called out.

"Sure."

The click of the deadbolt sent a zing of awareness through her. *Alone.* She could feel it from the roots of her hair to the tips of her toes and all the special places in between.

He could, too, or he wouldn't have barreled through the kitchen with a curt nod in her direction. In no time, he was across the back porch, out the door and down the wooden steps.

Opening her beer, she carried it out to the porch and stood where she could watch him. His arm seemed to move more easily as he scattered seed for the chickens. Splitting logs probably had warmed up his shoulder muscles although he'd been an idiot to ignore everyone's advice. If he weren't such a magnificent specimen hardened by ten years of military service, he would have paid the price for that idiocy.

That was Ryker, though, determined to prove that he was tough and resilient, especially after revealing what he considered a weakness. Leigh had him pegged. She had April pegged, too. Now that he'd ended his military career, she'd foolishly nourished the hope that he'd get over his superhero mindset and take a more measured approach to life. Judging from today, it wasn't likely.

Action in the yard switched to the goat pen. The princesses greeted their new best friend with enthusiasm, but of course they would because he'd brought them...no, wait. He wasn't carrying a pail of food, which meant they were excited about the soccer ball drill. Amazing.

He played with them for quite a while, long enough for her to leisurely sip two-thirds of her beer. When he gathered them into a huddle and made sure to scratch each goat's head, she got a little misty-eyed. If his plane was ready tomorrow, that would be the last they'd ever see of him, poor girls.

She took her beer into the living room and plopped down on the sofa. He'd be coming back after he fed the princesses and she didn't want to be caught staring through the screen looking as star-struck as those three goats. Even if she was.

Nobody lit her fire the way he did. She'd made a deal with herself. If he could say goodnight, walk into Leigh's bedroom and close the door, she wouldn't tell him what she had in her pockets. But if he hesitated, if he lingered at all, she just might.

<u>11</u>

After closing the princesses in for the night, Ryker walked back to the house. Slowly. April clearly objected to his plan of staying away from each other. He wasn't entirely sure if that meant she wanted to talk so they could mend fences or if she was thinking of...something else.

He was thinking of that something else, too. But he was too old for a long involved make-out session and that was all they could have. Yes, they could both achieve a certain amount of satisfaction that way, but the idea hit him wrong. Last night he'd been stressed out by the fireworks and ready to accept whatever was offered.

Not now. He wasn't willing to settle for crumbs tonight, which meant he'd go hungry. That was best all the way around. If he and April had been thrown together for a reason, it wasn't to make love or condoms would have miraculously appeared.

But the moment he opened the door and crossed the porch, his body began to tingle and his cock swelled in anticipation. Not good, but he didn't have to give in to instinct. He was a man, not a stallion sniffing out a mare in heat.

Damned if he could resist the urge to locate her, though. He wouldn't stay, but he had to know where she was. Then he could avoid her.

He was feeding himself lies, but they temporarily soothed him as he continued his search for April. She wasn't in the kitchen. Maybe he should grab a beer while he was here because once he closed himself in his room he couldn't come wandering out for drinks and snacks. That would negate the entire program.

Too bad it was so nice outside, though. Early evening in summer was one of his favorite times, when the fading light was gentle and the breezes warm. He wasn't happy about hibernating in his room but it couldn't be helped.

After twisting off the beer cap, he found the recycling bin and threw it inside. If that was the wrong place for it, Kevin would sort it out. He'd said they recycled everything unless they could reuse it and reusing a bottle cap made no sense.

He took a few swallows, hoping that would quench the fire raging inside him. No luck. He hung his hat on the back of a kitchen chair before continuing his search. He found her nestled into the sofa in the fuchsia and purple living room. He should have expected her to be there surrounded by colors that spoke to the primitive drumming of his heart.

She'd taken off her sandals and put her feet up. The sofa was generously sized and she'd created a nest of fuchsia and purple throw pillows. She gazed at him. "I see you changed your mind about the beer."

"Thought I'd take it to my room."

"You don't have to. The only chair in Leigh's room is a wobbly antique."

"I noticed that last night."

"If you want to relax with a beer, that one's better." She motioned to a large easy chair across from her that was slipcovered in fuchsia and purple swirls.

He evaluated the setup. The chair did look comfortable compared to what he'd find in Leigh's room. He'd rather not sit up in bed drinking a beer. He might accidentally spill some.

Taking a seat in the easy chair violated his original plan to avoid her once he fed the animals, but he'd be more than eight feet away. A respectable distance and there was even a coffee table between the chair and the sofa.

He lowered himself into the chair. Yeah, cushy. But the aroma of incense was stronger than he remembered from when they'd walked into the house. "Did you light some incense?"

"Just one stick. Mom has a habit of lighting one stick when she comes in here to wind down and not doing it seemed wrong."

"She unwinds in a fuchsia and purple room?"

"Maybe these days it's not so much unwinding as energizing. I can't honestly say I've been unwinding since I came in here. The energy's awesome, though, and I'm thinking it's the vibrancy of the paint. Can you feel it?"

Yes. But it was a figment of his imagination, a product of his fevered brain. They'd had this argument years ago and he'd stick with what he'd said back then. "You can't feel color. You might react emotionally to it, but you can't feel it."

"Nonsense." She put her empty bottle on the coffee table, stood and held up her arms. "That fuchsia is pulsing all around me, and the purple is drifting over my skin like crepe paper streamers."

"Is that your first beer?"

"Yep." She gave a little shimmy of joy. "I'm not drunk. It's the effect of being here with you in this color-drenched room. I've faced the truth, Ryker. We'll never get along except when we're naked, but for the next few hours that's good enough for me." Undulating her body in a sinuous dance, she approached his chair. "Want to change your mind about hiding in your room?"

His chest heaved and his balls tightened, but he shook his head. "I'm not a teenager anymore. Last night I was desperate for whatever we could have, but tonight I'm not willing to settle for less than everything. And we can't have that."

Digging in her pockets, she threw four little packets into his lap. "Guess again, cowboy."

"What the hell?"

"Compliments of my sister."

"Why?"

"She said we'd never have a productive conversation unless we got this out of the way first."

"Damn." He gazed up at her. "Do you think that's true?"

"Probably not."

"So even if we use all of them, we'll still be at square one?"

"Yes. But if we don't use any of them, we'll also be at square one and we'll have missed out on a chance to have one last hurrah before we give up on this fantasy."

He put down his beer, scooped up the packets and stood. His vocal cords weren't working great but he did his best. "Excellent logic." He shoved the condoms in his pocket and reached for her.

"I should hope so." She slid into his arms with the effortless grace of familiarity. "I have debate trophies."

Heart pounding so fast he could barely breathe, he gazed down at her. "If we're never doing this again, we need to make it count, make it memorable."

"That's a given. It'll be memorable regardless of—"

"I know, but I want...are there blankets we can throw on the ground?"

"What ground?"

"Get the blankets and I'll show you."

"Okay." She wiggled out of his arms. "Be right back."

He paced while he waited because standing still would have been impossible. After being plagued with indecision, he was taut and ready for this challenge. If making love to her tonight was a colossal mistake, and it very well could be, then too bad. He'd committed and there was no turning back. He was all in.

She showed up with several folded quilts in her arms. They looked as if they'd seen better days. "These are what Mom always uses for picnics."

"That's perfect. Let me carry them." He took the bundle. "We're going out back."

"You want to have sex in the backyard?"

"Not just in the backyard. I have a special place in mind." He followed her through the kitchen. When they reached the back porch, his boots thumped on the wood floor but her steps were silent. "I forgot that you're barefoot. Want to get shoes?"

"Nah, I like going barefoot."

He set the quilts on the table and sat in one of the wooden chairs. "Good idea." After pulling off his boots and socks, he stood and picked up the quilts. "Let's go."

She started toward the screen door. "It's funny, but I thought once you knew we had condoms you'd grab me and we'd do it on the nearest available surface."

"Then you don't know me as well as you think you do." He reached over her head so he could hold the door open for her.

"I just remember the way it used to be in the bed of your truck. There wasn't much planning involved back then. Just doing."

"Like I said, I'm not a teenager anymore." But as he descended the steps to the yard, the heaviness in his groin and the fizzy sensation in his veins were the same as they'd been eleven years ago. He could control it better now. Once upon a time he'd been confident he'd have a lifetime of nights with April. Now he was down to one.

She paused and turned to him. "Now what?"

Tucking the quilts under one arm, he took her hand. "This way." The grass tickled his feet. How long had it been since he'd walked barefoot through soft grass? Years.

"We're doing it in a vegetable garden?"

"Not just a vegetable garden. One in the shape of a peace symbol."

She sucked in a breath and her grip tightened. "Please don't be charming."

"*Please don't be charming*? What kind of BS is that?"

She tugged him to a stop and looked up, the soft glow of twilight reflected in her eyes. "I can go along with memorable if that means full-out, no-holds barred, lusty sex like we used to have." She swallowed. "But when it comes to you, I'm not prepared to handle special and significant."

Which was what, like a fool, he'd been going for. Would he never learn? Pain arrowed through his heart. He shoved it aside and let anger flow in. "Then forget the vegetable garden." He tossed the quilts to the ground, grabbed the top one and spread it out. "Here is fine."

"Ryker—"

"You're absolutely right. I don't know what I was thinking." He shook out a second quilt and laid it on top of the first. There was a third one but two was enough. "You said it earlier. One last hurrah.

One last chance to get naked." He stripped off his t-shirt, balled it up and spiked it into the grass.

"I don't want to have angry sex."

"Why not? We're good at that, too, as I recall." He unbuttoned his jeans.

"But it only works if we're both angry."

He paused, his fingers on the zipper tab, and took a long, slow breath. Damn it, he was being an ass. "Right again." Abandoning his undressing routine, he walked toward her. "This is more complicated than I thought."

She met his gaze. "Doesn't have to be."

He took a minute to digest the wisdom of those words. "That makes you three for three. Like I said, you're the smart one around here." He drew her into his arms. "How about if we back up the bus and start over?"

"Great plan." She relaxed against him and wound her arms around his neck. "What's next?"

"We get horizontal. Easier to kiss each other." Lifting her up, he carried her to the quilt bed and laid her down. Then he stretched out on his side and scooped her in close. He still had enough light to see the familiar contours of her heart-shaped face and the tiny gold flecks in her brown eyes. Typical eighteen-year-old, he used to think he knew everything there was to know about April Harris.

He'd been wrong then and he'd be even more wrong now. Slowly he traced the arch of her brows, the curve of her cheekbones, the slope of her nose and the velvet texture of her lips. "You look the same, and yet not."

"I think my face used to be more rounded looking."

"Maybe that's it. Now you're more defined."

She rubbed her hand along his jaw. "You are, too, although you've always seemed to be carved from granite." She touched the scar on his cheek, the one that most people didn't even notice. "How'd you get this?"

"Are you sure you want to know?"

"Now that you mention it, no, I don't. I'd rather have you kiss me."

"I was just getting to that." As he slipped his hand behind her neck, her beaded earring brushed the back of his wrist. Moving with deliberation, he captured her beautiful mouth.

She yielded to him like a wildflower to sunshine. Dizzy with pleasure, he explored with his tongue, shifted his angle and sank deeper into the kiss. So perfect. And he'd almost messed it up. Gratitude washed away the last of his pain and anger.

As the kiss generated more heat, her clothes became an annoyance he could do without. Sliding his hand under her shirt, he unhooked her bra.

She made a noise of protest, grasped his face in both hands and eased away from the kiss. "Hang on, there, cowboy."

"I thought you wanted—"

"I do." She gulped for air. "But let's change things up. Lie back." Her throaty command was followed by a firm shove.

The move was unexpected and he toppled right over like an obedient puppy.

"That's better." She hooked her leg around his hip and slid on top of him. "I swore if we ended up doing this the dynamic would change." She took another quick breath. "Then you kissed me and I forgot."

"You don't like the dynamic?"

"I used to love it." Straddling him just above his package, she flattened her hands against his chest and pushed herself to a sitting position. Then she paused to take another breath. "You were the big strong guy who could pick me up and carry me around. I let you do that last night. And again, just now. Old habits die hard."

"I thought you liked me to carry you around."

"Sometimes, sure. Not *all* the time."

"Now I know." That info's usefulness would expire in about twelve hours, but he'd keep it in mind until then.

"And I also like being on top." She whipped off her shirt and bra and tossed them aside.

He gulped. She was magnificent. And her tattoo, symbolizing love and nurturing, was right where it should be. Reaching for her, he cradled a satin-smooth breast in each hand and squeezed gently. His cock pressed hard against his fly. "I would have been happy to let you be on top."

"I wasn't very evolved. You taking charge thrilled me."

"So I'm not supposed to take charge tonight?" In that case, he hoped she'd get this convoy rolling soon.

"Not this time. Maybe next time."

Right. Four condoms meant three more next times, not counting fooling around. The way his body was vibrating with anticipation, it was a wonder she wasn't jiggling around up there. "When do you estimate this one will get going?"

She leaned forward, pressing her breasts into his hands. "How about now?"

Heat shot straight to his privates. "Sounds good."

"You'll have to turn me loose, though." She gently removed his hands from her breasts and changed her position to the far side of the bulge in his Wranglers.

She contemplated it for a few seconds while he struggled to accept his new passive role. He didn't like it. There was a reason he'd trained to be a pilot and not a co-pilot.

But when she reached for his zipper, he suddenly had an important job—not coming. If he lost focus and she wasn't careful, they'd both be in trouble. "Take it easy as you pull that down."

Her eyebrows lifted. "Is that an order?"

"Let me *suggest* that you take it easy as you pull that down."

"Don't worry. I will."

"Ever been pranked with a pop-up snake in a nut can?"

She started to laugh.

"It's not going to be that funny, but it might be that dramatic."

"You're wearing boxers, though, so there's some containment involved."

"Yes, and I...oh, hell. They're those flimsy peace symbol boxers. They won't contain me worth a damn."

She doubled over, giggling and holding her sides. "I forgot about those boxers! Oh, Lord, Ryker."

Although he appreciated the sight of her sweet dancing breasts when she laughed, this was *not* how he'd wanted things to go, with her getting hysterical over his dorky boxers. Lifting his torso, he propped himself on his elbows. "Move aside and let me up. I'll take everything off myself."

"Where's the fun in that?" She stayed put and cleared her throat. "Lie down and remember who's in charge. I can do this."

"With a straight face?"

"Is that a requirement?"

With a sigh, he flopped back onto the quilt and gestured toward his fly. "It's all yours. Go for it."

"Now you have the idea." She slowly drew down the zipper.

He closed his eyes, both because he was battling an impending climax and because he didn't want to see her expression when she uncovered peace symbols in a rainbow of colors. Relief at having the zipper down was countered by an image of decorated underwear covering his privates. He probably looked like an effing circus tent down there.

He'd love to know her plan but asking might be a violation of his new set of orders. When her warm fingers curled around his straining bad boy, he shuddered.

Gradually, tenderly, she worked his pocket rocket through the front opening of his boxers. Maybe she'd dig out one of the condoms, now, which would be A-OK with him. He didn't have to be completely undressed to make this work. Instead she flicked her tongue against the very tip of his cock...and took it in her mouth.

He no longer gave a damn about stupid underwear.

12

April hadn't planned to start off with oral sex, but as Ryker panted and moaned in response to her ministrations, she concluded it was the perfect way to launch tonight's adventure. As teenagers, they'd been willing to experiment but they hadn't been very accomplished. Maybe she was guilty of showing off tonight, but she'd learned a few things since then. She wanted him to know it.

She'd have been willing to commit to a grand oral sex finale, too. But when he gripped her by the shoulders and lifted her away from his cock, she didn't resist. She'd made her point.

His voice sounded like a rusty file scraping on metal. "That was great."

"Good."

"But I want…"

Clearly he wasn't used to asking. She braced her hands on his chest again and leaned down, her mouth a breath away from his. "Tell me."

He cupped the back of her head. "I'd show you, but I'm not in charge." Then he pulled her into a hot, demanding kiss.

The fire in that kiss tempted her to hand over the control. She didn't. Slowly she eased back from his seductive mouth. "Tell me what you want."

His breath hitched. "To be deep inside you."

"I can make that happen." She brushed her lips over his. "You don't have to do anything but lie here and enjoy."

"That's not my style. I'm—"

"And breathe." Leaving him with one last feathery kiss, she scooted down and peeled off his jeans and boxers. Then she stripped off the rest of her clothes and plucked a condom out of his jeans pocket.

He clutched sections of the quilt in each fist and groaned through gritted teeth as she rolled it on. Trembling with anticipation, she straddled his hips and flattened her palms on his heaving chest.

This was it. Because she didn't want to add significance, she closed her eyes instead of gazing into his. She was drenched, which made the process easy, but she'd forgotten how completely he filled her. She'd forgotten the impact of holding his strength and power inside her body, and how quickly the sensation ignited her eager response.

She moved slowly, relearning all those things as the pressure increased. She'd meant to tease him a little, play a game of cat and mouse, demonstrate that she could wield power, too. There would be none of that. She was about to lose her mind.

He gasped out her name.

Opening her eyes, she met his gaze.

The fading light couldn't blunt the intensity of his expression, the heat in his blue eyes. He circled her hips with his big hands, his fingers pressing, insistent.

As if at his bidding, she came apart. With a cry of surrender, she abandoned herself to a whirlwind of sensory overload followed by his primal roar of pleasure. Gripping her thighs, he thrust upward and pulsed within her. It was done.

She remained braced above him, her head down and her breathing ragged. Beneath her palms, his chest rose and fell rapidly and his skin was damp with sweat. He continued to hold onto her thighs but his grip had loosened. She peeked quickly at his face. His eyes were closed.

Over the years she'd convinced herself that making love to Ryker hadn't been particularly special. Either she'd been kidding herself or their eleven-year separation had created this firestorm. Might be a little of both. Whatever the explanation, she was wiped out.

Blowing out a breath, he slid both hands over her hips and up her back, where he exerted gentle pressure. "Come here."

If she hadn't been so shaky she might have put up a fuss about what sounded suspiciously like a command. So much was coming back to her, like the fact he liked to cuddle after making love.

A good climax tended to make him chatty, which was fine if they avoided discussing the epic nature of their mutual orgasm. She relaxed her arms and sank down, resting her cheek on his shoulder and her upper body on his chest. Nice. She'd always loved the combination of springy chest hair and moist skin that was Ryker after sex. "This reminds me of Child's Pose."

"What's that?" He stroked her back.

"A yoga pose."

"Oh. Never took yoga."

"What a surprise."

"Would I like it?"

"Maybe some parts." His easy caress had a hypnotic affect and her eyes drifted closed. "The strength-based poses. But mostly it keeps you limber."

"I don't remember you doing yoga before."

"Leigh and I started going to a class in Kalispell. I'm sure yoga helped with her pregnancy."

He was quiet for a while. "I didn't get to see much of Pax today."

She started to say that was because he'd spent so much time chopping wood, but she changed her mind. "Do you wish you had?"

"Yeah."

Interesting. "Have Mandy and Zane talked about having kids?"

"Not yet, but they probably will. Hope so. That would be fun." He increased the range of his caress to include her ass and his stroking changed to fondling.

"What are you doing?"

"Enjoying myself. I think you have some extra padding that wasn't there eleven years ago."

"Hey!" She pushed up and glared at him. "That's not a nice thing to say to a lady."

"I meant it as a compliment." He began a sensuous massage. "I like how you feel. Is it my turn to be in charge?"

"If you have to ask, then the answer is no."

"Then let me rephrase. It's my turn to be in charge." He flipped her neatly to her back while keeping them tightly connected.

She only had time for a quick gasp of surprise before he disengaged and stood. The guy had possessed ninja reflexes in high school and he'd obviously honed them in the years since.

"That first time was terrific but it didn't last long enough to suit me." He disposed of the condom. "I don't know about you, but I'm ready for another round."

"I can see that." Moonlight gave her an excellent view of how ready he was. A naked, muscled god stood before her. What an idiot she'd been to think she could ever tame a man like Ryker McGavin.

"Yes, but does it interest you?"

"Greatly."

"All I need to know." He opened another condom packet, tossed the foil on the quilt and rolled on the condom in one efficient movement. When he dropped to his knees beside her, his breath caught. "You know, when I look at you lying there all mussed and willing, I can't help thinking that—"

"Four won't be enough?" Maybe he hadn't been about to say something that would take them into dangerous territory, but she didn't want to chance it.

His slight hesitation spoke volumes. "Exactly." He moved over her and lowered his mouth to hers.

His kiss was blatantly sexual as if to emphasize what this night was about. He nibbled on her lips and thrust his tongue deep with a suggestive rhythm. Then he directed his attention to her earlobe. He'd once teased her that she wore long, dangling earrings as a signal that she loved being touched there. Then he'd tested his theory and proved it correct.

No one had guessed her ears were a powerful erogenous zone except him. Years ago, he'd been fascinated by that. Judging from his behavior, he still was. When he unhooked her earring and began to nip and lick her lobe, she squirmed against the quilt.

His warm breath tickled that sensitive spot. "Bet I can still make you come." While he continued to nuzzle behind her ear and use his tongue on the delicate inner shell, he dragged her earring slowly back and forth over her breasts.

He'd discovered the sensual trick by accident and it had never failed to arouse her. Her nipples tightened into aching buds and her thighs grew slick.

When she began to whimper, he urged her on with a low, seductive murmur. "Let go. You know you want to. Come for me."

She gulped for air. "You're a devil."

"And you love it."

"*Yes.*"

"Climax time." Dropping the earring between her breasts, he pinched her nipple at the same time he thrust his tongue in her ear.

She came in a rush, arching off the quilt and panting.

He blew softly on her damp ear. "Well done."

"Didn't...think...you'd remember."

"Ah, but I did." Retrieving her earring, he carefully slipped the hook through her lobe. Then he brushed her lips with his. "I had to find out if you still reacted that way."

"I do."

"I noticed."

"But you're the only one who knows."

"Is that so?" He sounded pleased.

"Don't let it go to your head."

"It's going in an entirely different direction." He settled between her thighs. "Hang on and I'll show you." With one deliberate thrust, he buried his cock deep.

She gave an involuntary sigh of pleasure. Ryker had been given a gift and he knew how to use it.

He chuckled. "Like that?"

"I'm not going to inflate your ego by answering."

"Why not? You've already inflated my cock, so you might as well give me an ego to match."

"I think it already does, flyboy."

"Oh, them's fightin' words, ma'am." He began a slow, steady rhythm.

That movement, so deceptively simple and straightforward, touched off little explosions of happiness with every stroke. "You don't like being called a flyboy?"

"That's not the problem." He maintained the pace as if it cost him no effort at all. "You've implied that I'm an arrogant flyboy. The correct description is confident flyboy."

"My mistake." Any minute now she'd lose track of the conversation. He'd been able to reduce her to a hot mess years ago and he was better at it, now.

Supporting himself on his forearms, he leaned closer as he continued to pump. "Then you'll take it back?"

"Sure." She was willing to say whatever he wanted if he'd just keep on doing what he was doing. She was ramping up to a high that promised to end in a spectacular fashion.

"April."

"What?" His soft voice barely registered because the blood flowing through her body had mostly gathered where warmth and friction were creating something great. She wrapped her legs around his muscular thighs to tighten the connection. Oh, yeah, that was *good*.

"The thing is, I—"

"Hm?"

"Nothing." He bore down and stroked faster. "Buckle up. We're coming in for a landing." Sliding his hands under her hips, he lifted her to change the angle as he drove home.

She welcomed her release with a shout of joy. Submerged in the heat of a glorious, full-body climax, she called his name.

"I'm here." His voice was hoarse with passion. "Right here." With a loud groan, he thrust once more and held her fast as his big body trembled.

She wrapped him in her arms and absorbed the shockwaves of his orgasm as they melded with hers. Gradually her breathing slowed and her heart no longer beat in double time. She lay in Ryker's arms saturated with the kind of contentment that had eluded her for years. Eleven, to be exact.

But try as she might, she couldn't hold onto her orgasmic bliss. Already it was slipping away. This crazy sexual interlude had sounded so logical as she'd sat in her mother's fuchsia and purple living room sipping beer. Yet blowing off steam made no sense if she continued to fan the flame under the pressure cooker.

Bottom line, she wasn't comfortable having sex without context no matter how hard she tried to convince herself she could handle it. Mindless sex wasn't in his wheelhouse, either. He'd tried to set up their lovemaking in the peace garden. At least once tonight he'd seemed ready to talk seriously about their situation.

Leigh firmly believed they had to clear the sexual tension away before they could have any kind of healing discussion. Well, they'd done that. They'd used half the condoms. Maybe, instead of continuing to have sex while they avoided talking about anything meaningful, they should take a risk and open the channels of communication.

About the time she'd decided that, he lifted his head and gazed down at her. "Are you okay?"

"Yep." She rubbed his back. "Just thinking."

"About what?"

There it was, her opening. She'd been the one to lay out the rules and the one to remind him of them when he'd strayed from the designated path. She'd have to be the one to change them. "I thought we could just have sex and let it go at that, but...it's like I've shut off part of myself. I'm censoring what I think, what I say."

"I know the feeling."

"Maybe Leigh's right. We needed to have sex first, but now we need to talk."

He greeted that with silence.

"Ryker?"

"I'm thinking."

"Okay. Carry on with that."

At last he heaved a sigh. "I suppose it's a good idea."

"But you don't want to?"

"I'd rather take a kick in the balls."

"Then maybe—"

"But I've been censoring myself, too. If we'd just met, then a night of sex with no strings could work. For us, it's impossible without playing mind games. I'm not good at those."

"So you *do* want to talk about it?"

"Yeah, I guess. We can see how it goes."

"Maybe we should grab a couple of beers."

He hesitated. "Did you want to go inside?"

"Not necessarily."

"Good. I'd rather stay out here." He eased away from her and stood. "I'll fetch the beer."

"All right. Thanks." She sat up and reached for the extra quilt. The breeze was cool, but she liked the idea of having their discussion under the stars. "Snacks would be good, too. They keep chips and stuff in the cupboard over the sink. See what you can find."

"I'll check it out." He pulled on his jeans. "Be right back."

"Thanks for doing this."

He turned and walked backward. "You bet. Anything else you want me to bring?"

"I meant thanks for being willing to talk."

He paused and took a deep breath. "It's time." Then he turned and jogged toward the house.

Her heart ached as she watched him go. He'd always been brave, sometimes foolishly so. But this discussion would take a different brand of courage. He might have volunteered for the beer run so he'd have time alone to prepare.

_13_

During Ryker's time in the military, he'd adopted a method for dealing with dicey situations. He'd ask himself what was the worst that could happen so he was prepared for that eventuality. In battle, that could include friends dying and ultimately him dying.

This upcoming discussion with April didn't involve physical danger. He should find that comforting. He didn't. His gut still churned as he took two bottles of beer from the fridge, opened them and set them on the counter.

He stood in front of the open kitchen cupboard debating the chip selection much longer than necessary. Yeah, he was stalling. Okay, what was the worst that could happen? They'd get in a big fight and say terrible things to each other, worse than what they'd said eleven years ago.

Instead of healing old wounds, they'd open new ones. Despite living in the same small town, they'd avoid each other like the plague. Nobody would die, but it might seem like a kind of death. Worry about running into her would tarnish his joy at being back home.

Well, then, if he saw that kind of fight developing, he'd walk away from it. Simple as that. He grabbed a bag of potato chips, closed the cupboard, and picked up both beers. Showtime.

She was bundled up in the spare quilt when he got back. They used to snuggle under a blanket in the back of his truck as the weather cooled. He'd managed to suppress that kind of memory while he was away, but he couldn't do it anymore after spending two days with her.

He gave her the chips. "Hope these work."

"My favorite kind." She opened the bag and propped it against her knee. "Thanks. I can take my beer, now."

He dropped down beside her and handed over her beer. "Well, here we are. How do you want to start?"

"I'm not sure. While you were gone, I was trying to decide how to structure it." She popped a chip into her mouth.

"*Structure* it? Are you sure we don't need a moderator and a slide presentation?"

"Cut it out, Ryker. Just simple things, like who goes first."

He chewed and swallowed a chip. "You do."

"Why?"

"You're a woman, so you—"

"Forget that nonsense! We'll draw straws."

"With what?

She glanced around and spied the foil condom wrappers. "I can make two straws out of one of these."

"Go for it."

She turned away from him. "Don't look."

"Do you honestly think I would?" Then he sighed. "Sorry. I'm...a little bit on edge."

"And I'm channeling my childhood with Leigh. She always tried to peek."

"I believe it." He took a sip of beer. "She used to spy on us from her bedroom window when I'd bring you home."

"She did? I don't remember that."

"Because you were all dreamy eyed and weren't paying attention."

"And you weren't dreamy eyed?"

"Not when I walked you to your front door. I stayed alert."

"Because of my sister?"

"No, she just happened to be one of the things I noticed. Mostly I was watching for anything that might startle you."

She gazed at him. "I never realized you were on guard."

"Habit."

"Are you on guard, now?"

"Sure."

"Would you rather go inside so you don't have to be?"

He shook his head. "I love being outdoors. Always have. But I pay attention. Been doing that all my life."

She tossed the strips of foil on the blanket. "Forget drawing straws. You should start. Tell me why you enlisted."

His stomach clenched. "I told you why eleven years ago. You didn't buy it."

"Tell me again." She took a breath. "Please."

"I'm grateful to be living in this country and enlisting in the service was a way to contribute, to give back."

"There are other ways to do that, ways that don't put your life at risk."

It would be so easy to get upset over her implication that he should have simply picked a safer career. Instead he took a deep breath and let the comment go. "The Air Force appealed to me."

"Why? I mean other than wanting to fly jets. I kind of get that."

"You don't get to fly fighter jets unless you enlist in the military." He sipped his beer. "When I was a kid I set my heart on being a pilot like my dad. You've known that about me since we met. Why are you still baffled by my choice?"

"Because it's one thing to plan something so daring when you're unattached. But by the time you were old enough to follow through, you were in love with me, or at least that's what you said."

His jaw tightened. "Are you questioning whether I loved you?"

She took a long, slow breath. "Sorry. That last part was unfair. It's just hard for me to understand how you could love me and then head into battle where you could be killed."

"I saw it as protecting our way of life, which ultimately protects the ones I love, including you." He held onto his temper with difficulty.

"By sacrificing yourself?"

"If necessary."

She gazed at him. "And we all would have lost you." Her voice trembled and she paused to clear her throat. "Me, your mom, your brothers, your friends."

Her emotional response tore him up, but if he could get her to see the big picture, maybe they could make some progress. "Every soldier has loved ones, April," he said gently. "All the soldiers I've known felt the same as me, that this was something they were doing for the country and for their families, because they were suited to a soldier's life and others might not be."

"Even if the families don't want them to go in?"

"Even then. I was blessed with a strong body, fast reflexes and excellent eyesight. Not to brag, but I made a damned good soldier."

She swallowed. "I'm sure you did."

"I knew all along it was the right thing for me, even if you, Mom and my brothers didn't. Enlisting in the Air Force meant I was making the best use of my talents."

"Then why come home now?"

"When I compared my performance to the twenty-year-olds, I was a hair's-breadth slower in my reaction time. That gap would only get wider. I needed to pass the baton."

"And you'd do it all over again, wouldn't you?"

"Yep."

"Oh, Ryker." She sniffed and swiped at her eyes. "I understand wanting to contribute, but you could have died!"

"Some things are bigger than one person's life."

"That sounds so noble. Then I imagine you giving yours and I...I can't bear it."

"I can tell." He ached all over. She wasn't in very good shape, either. Moonlight picked up the sheen of tears on her cheeks. He started to put a comforting arm around her shoulders but reconsidered. Touching her might lead to making love again, but that would only apply a temporary patch to something that would never be permanently fixed.

They weren't yelling at each other the way they had eleven years ago when she ended the relationship, but in a way, this was worse. Discussing it was painful and pointless because the conclusion was always the same. She'd been right to end it. She couldn't accept the risks he was willing to take if he could make a difference. That was as true now as it had been when he'd enlisted.

He sighed. "This was a nice idea but it's not working out." Slowly he got to his feet. "We might as well go inside."

"You go ahead. I'd rather stay out here."

"All right." He moved to the far side of the quilt and sat down again.

"What are you doing?"

"If you're staying out here, so am I."

"Are you *guarding* me?"

"If you want to call it that."

"Well, don't do it, okay?" She wiped her eyes with the edge of the quilt.

She'd switched from sad crying to mad crying, so now if he tried to comfort her she'd only push him away. He shrugged. "It's part of my DNA."

"Well, you and your DNA can mosey on down the road, cowboy. I've managed to survive all this time without you watching over my every move. Borrow my mom's car if you want. The keys are in my backpack, top front pocket. Go out on the town."

"No, thanks." He took another swallow of his beer.

She stared at him. "Seriously? You're going to sit there because I don't want to come inside?"

"Yes."

"Oh, for pity's sake!" Gathering the quilt more tightly and holding onto her beer, she scrambled upright. "You win. We'll go inside. I certainly won't enjoy being out here with you sitting over there in stony silence."

"I could sing."

"Ryker, you are such a pain in the ass." She snatched up the chips and marched toward the house.

"So I've been told." He finished off his beer and set the bottle in the grass. Then he tossed her clothes and his t-shirt in the middle of the quilt bed, rolled it up and carried the bedroll and his empty bottle into the house.

Still wrapped in the quilt, April stood in the kitchen with her back to him. Her choked sobs gutted him. "Hey."

She turned to look at him with red-rimmed eyes.

He couldn't stand it. Crossing to her, he pulled her into his arms. "I'm so sorry we ended up like this."

"Me, too." She pressed her face against his chest.

"I mean it. This is your house. I'll stay in my room. You won't have to see me at all."

"That's impossible."

"No, it's not." He rubbed her back.

"Yes, it is." Her voice was muffled against his chest. "You may be a big tough soldier, but even soldiers have to pee if they drink beer."

"I suppose. Tell you what. I'll take you up on the loan of your Mom's car and get out of here for a little while."

She gulped. "Okay. Thanks, Ryker."

"You bet."

"I'll just...I'll just duck into my room until you're gone." Easing away from him, she gave him a little smile and a wave before heading down the hall in her quilt cocoon.

He quickly accomplished the tasks necessary before he could head out – putting on his shirt and boots, grabbing his hat and phone, locking the back door, turning out lights in the kitchen.

He made sure his wallet was still in his back pocket and located the keys in her backpack. Last he turned off lights in the living room and walked out the front door. Knob lock engaged, check. Deadbolt engaged, check.

On the way to the Prius he hit the button on the key fob to unlock the door. If his brothers could see him now, they'd split a gut. He was picky about what he drove, always had been. He didn't care so much about the outside, but he'd always insisted on a powerful engine that could haul some serious ass. This ride was so not him.

April had adjusted the driver's seat to her specs, so that had to change. But nothing could be done about the mannerly sound of the engine as he backed out of the drive. His GPS had given him the location of a neighborhood bar not too far away. As he pulled into a parking space, he glanced around. Not a single Prius except this one. Just pickups and a few SUVs. He was back among his peeps.

Music, laughter and guitar music greeted him as he walked through the door. It reminded him of the Guzzling Grizzly back home, although this place was bigger. A live band with a bass, a guitar and a fiddle belted out a classic George Strait tune. He thought of his little brother, who'd hung up his guitar after that disaster with his fiancée. He and Bryce hadn't been lucky in love, that was for sure.

The place was jumping, but he managed to snag the last empty stool at the bar. A laminated menu was stuck in a metal holder in front of him and he pulled it out. A quick glance told him he wasn't among vegetarians anymore.

The bartender was a woman with blond hair and a flirty manner. "What'll you have, cowboy?"

"A draft, please, ma'am. And a burger, well done."

"You want the single patty or the He-man with the double patty?"

"The He-man."

She grinned. "I figured. Fries?"

"Why not?"

"Coming up." She winked at him before she sashayed away.

She might be angling for a bigger tip, but he thought there could be more to it than that. He seemed to affect women that way.

She brought his beer, and the head of foam on that sucker was perfect. He thanked her.

"You here for the rodeo?"

"No, ma'am."

"Did you just move to town, then? I know most of the cowboys from this area and I don't recognize you."

"I'm visiting."

"But you're not participating in the rodeo?"

"No, ma'am. I operate a commuter airline out of Eagles Nest." He liked saying it. Yes, he had only one plane currently, but he'd expand, especially if he could talk Badger into flying with him.

Her eyes widened. "You're a *pilot*?"

"Yes, ma'am." He didn't consider himself ego-driven, but after what he'd just been through with April, the bartender's reaction soothed his soul.

"Misty!" someone called from the end of the bar. "We need some refills down here!"

"Be right there, Russell!"

The woman had pipes. Ryker's ears were still ringing after she left to take care of the cowboys at the end of the bar. He picked up his glass and was about to take a sip when a Stetson-wearing guy sitting next to him leaned in his direction. He looked to be late sixties, early seventies.

"Couldn't help listening in on your conversation with Misty. You run a commuter airline?"

"Yes, sir."

"How big are your planes?"

"We can accommodate six passengers. Seven if somebody wants to sit up front with me." He decided to say *we* because technically Badger's financial contribution made it a two-man operation.

"Sounds perfect for my poker buddies and me. Got a business card?"

"Sadly, I left them in my other pants."

"You don't have business cards yet, do you?"

"Not at the present time, but we're working on it. We should—"

"No worries." The guy took a cocktail napkin out of a holder at the bar and borrowed a pen from the person next to him. "I like giving business to startups. We need more of that can-do attitude in this country. Give me your website."

He heaved a sigh of relief. Thanks to the efforts of Zane's fiancée Mandy, he had a website. He rattled off BadgerAirlines.com.

"Badger?" His new friend laughed. "Why not name it something to do with flight? Like maybe eagles or hawks? Last time I checked, badgers don't fly."

Ryker grinned. "I happen to know one who flies F-15s."

"I knew it!" The guy pointed his borrowed pen at Ryker. "You're ex-military. I can spot 'em a mile away."

"Or a few inches away."

"That, too." He stuck out his hand. "Frank Bledsoe."

Ryker shook his hand. "Ryker McGavin."

"Pleased to meet you, Ryker. I have four buddies who've been pestering me about setting up a fishing trip in your area before it gets too damned cold. If you'd come fetch us and take us back home, that would facilitate things nicely. These guys would love the idea of flying with a vet."

Ryker blinked. "That would make a difference?"

"Are you kidding? We all served back in the day. It would be an honor to fly with you, Ryker." He clapped him on the back. "Nice meeting you, but I have to take off. Need to pick up my wife from bingo. Never did care for that game, so while she plays, I drink. You'll be hearing from me."

"Great!"

"One He-man Burger for the cowboy in the straw hat." Misty set the plate in front of him. "Can I get you another draft?"

He'd been so involved with Frank that he'd barely touched the first one. "Thanks, but I'm good."

She chuckled. "I'll bet you are."

Another time, another place, he might have picked up on that. Instead he let the comment go and tucked into his burger. Delicious. Much as he enjoyed April's family, he couldn't imagine going the rest of his life without having a burger or a steak now and then.

After he polished off both the beer and the meal, he left a generous tip for Misty and slipped out of the bar while she was busy with other customers. He hadn't wanted to stay at the bar any longer, but he wasn't ready for bed, either. The chance meeting with Frank had energized him.

Using his status as a vet to bring business to his airline hadn't been on his radar, but why not? If Badger came on board, the airline would have two ex-military pilots. A couple of other guys from the squadron had shown interest when he and Badger had been making plans. This thing could grow.

Keys in hand, he walked out to the silent parking lot. But as he hit the button on the keychain, a pop sounded overhead. Then another and another. The sky filled with light and the air vibrated with sound.

He braced himself and waited for a repeat of last night's anxiety attack. Several more rockets shot into the sky over his head and erupted into a sparkling cascade of color. Gradually he relaxed. He was okay. He didn't picture bombs falling and buildings disintegrating. He didn't imagine a long casualty list or a crowded medical tent.

He didn't know if April was in a better place because they'd separated for a little while, but he certainly was. He wasn't likely to find out what mood she was in, either, because he'd given her plenty of time to settle in and fall asleep. He climbed into the Prius, started the engine and left a parking lot that continued to be dominated by pickups and SUVs.

Aimless driving around would be a waste of gas and wasn't what he wanted, either. Ideally he'd have someone he could tell about this new development and what it could mean for the future.

But anyone who cared was either on the other side of the world flying F-15s or in Eagles Nest getting ready for bed. It was too late to be calling his mom or his brothers.

Might as well get some shuteye. But when he pulled into the driveway next to the Harris' turquoise house, all the lights he'd turned off were back on. It looked like April was awake.

14

When the Prius pulled into the driveway, April turned off her music and put a bookmark in her mystery. Ryker had been gone for less time than she'd expected, but she'd been prepared to wait no matter how late he stayed out. She had something to say.

When the car door closed, she got up and tightened the sash on her robe. Then she walked to the door, unlocked it and swung it open. "I'm awake."

He climbed the steps to the front porch. "I can see that." His gaze flicked over her. "Did you sleep at all?"

"No." She stepped away from the door so he could come in. "I meant to go straight to bed after I finished the chips and beer, but then I decided to take a shower and I had an epiphany from the negative ions."

He frowned in confusion. "A whozit from the whatzit?"

"An epiphany from the negative ions. You don't remember that from our physical science class?"

"I was too busy watching you take notes and chew on your tongue."

She sighed. "That's such an annoying habit and I can't seem to stop doing it."

"I think it's cute."

"I think it's dumb." But talking about her silly behavior helped calm her nerves. She gestured toward the easy chair. "Would you be willing to stay for a bit so I can tell you about my epiphany?"

"Sure."

"Can I get you anything?"

"No thanks." He took off his hat and laid it on the small table next to the chair. "I had a beer and a burger."

"I'll bet you did. Have the vegetarian meals been driving you crazy?"

"Not at all." He waited until she sat on the couch before lowering himself into the chair. "Everything's tasted great." He propped his booted foot on his knee. "I was just in the mood for a burger."

"Then I'm glad you treated yourself to one." It was like seeing him for the first time. The hem of his jeans was starting to fray and his boots were scuffed. That was so Ryker. He'd always been casual about clothes and intense about jets and the military. He'd told her exactly who he was. She just hadn't listened.

"So what's this negative ion—epiphany thing I apparently missed in science class?"

"It's fairly simple. People can have aha moments when they're around water, especially falling water, because it produces negative ions that improve your mood and boost your creativity."

"Well, damn. I wish I'd paid attention. That would have come in handy a time or two." He gazed at her, caution in his blue eyes. "So what's your brainstorm?"

She hesitated. While she'd waited for him to come back, she'd rehearsed this part in her head but now that he was here she was losing her nerve. "Please don't take this the wrong way."

"Oh, boy. Here it comes." He put both feet on the floor and braced his big hands on his knees. "Nobody ever starts out like that unless they're ready to hit you with a doozy."

"I don't want to hit you with anything. But...I had this thought and it resonates with me."

"Then you might as well spit it out."

"Okay." She took a breath to steady herself. "We should never have dated in the first place."

The flash of pain in his eyes was quickly snuffed out. "What makes you say that?"

"Think about it. I was the girl who plastered her locker with bumper stickers like *Make Love, Not War*. You were the guy who'd memorized the dialogue from *Top Gun*. We never had a chance."

"Then why did you go out with me?"

"Because I thought you were sexy. You turned me on. What about you? Why did you ask me out?"

"Same reason. I'd see you walking down the hall with your girlfriends and I just...wanted you. And for the record, that part hasn't changed."

"Not for me, either." She held his gaze and the air between them crackled with tension.

He broke the connection and ran his fingers through his short hair. "So that's your epiphany? That we should have nipped this thing in the bud? Because unless you have a time machine we can't fix that mistake."

"No, but I can fix the way I've been dealing with it. Something Leigh said today's been nagging me because it's so true." She paused to gather her courage before looking straight into his eyes. He deserved that. "Ever since our first date, our first kiss, I've been hoping you'd change."

He stared at her. Then he swallowed. "Yes, you have."

Her chest tightened. "I'm sorry, Ryker. That was so wrong of me and so unfair to you."

"Yeah, well..." Leaning forward, he rested his arms on his knees and bowed his head. "On some level I've always known you can't accept me the way I am." Then he looked up. "But thank you for saying it. That couldn't have been easy."

How beautifully he'd handled her confession. But she'd be damned if she'd start crying again. "No, it wasn't easy." She stood and tightened the sash on her robe. "But I needed to say it. Goodnight, Ryker." She started out of the living room.

"Don't go."

She paused, heart pounding as she fought to breathe. Footsteps. The air moved behind her. He was there.

But he didn't touch her. "Look, you're right about all of it. I've never been the guy you needed. I refused to admit it because I couldn't stand to give you up. I'm admitting it now. After tonight we'll call it quits for good. But...tonight's not over."

The combination of his emotion-filled words and the heat he generated ate at her resolve. "Having sex again is a mistake."

"We already made the big one by getting together in the first place. What's one more?"

She turned and gazed into his eyes. They reflected the same yearning that she was struggling to resist. She could make the noble choice and deny them both the pleasure they could find in each other's arms. Or she could surrender to her needs...and his.

As she began to tremble in anticipation, the choice became obvious. "Unless I've lost count, we can make two more mistakes."

"That's a big assumption. It's been a long day. I might not be capable of making two mistakes."

"I guess we'll find out." She slipped her hand into his. "Come with me."

His grip tightened. "Yes, ma'am."

He'd no sooner stepped into her bedroom than he had her out of her robe and stretched out on her bed while he kissed every inch of her quivering body. He stopped only long enough to strip off his own clothes and toss the remaining condoms on the bedside table.

He was naturally a take-charge kind of guy, a behavior that had thrilled her years ago. Even when they'd both been virgins, he'd seemed to know what she needed without asking. A full-steam ahead technique might not work for a less sexually aware man, but Ryker had instincts.

He was making use of them now. The sensuous slide of his lips and tongue combined with stroking from his talented fingertips left her moaning and gasping for breath. She'd thrashed around until the sheets and quilt were a tangled mess.

At one point, he pinned her to the mattress with his big body and peppered her face with kisses until she couldn't stop giggling.

"This is the same bed, isn't it?" He paused long enough to glance up at the headboard with its painted flowers. "The one we made love on when your family was at the movies."

She gulped in air. "Same one."

"Thought so." His gaze searched hers. "This is stupid, but please tell me that no other guy has made love to you in this bed."

"They haven't."

"Good." Heat flickered in his eyes. ""It was the first time I did this." He slid down between her thighs and proceeded to drive her insane. After the enthusiastic caresses that had led up to that move, making her come was ridiculously easy. Such glorious pleasure! She yelled until her throat hurt.

He kissed his way back to her mouth. "I think you liked that."

"Nah." She could hardly breathe, let alone speak. "I was...faking."

"Then get ready to fake some more." He reached for a condom. "I'm going to spend one of these and I want you to come, too."

"I'll do my best."

"That's good enough for me."

In moments, he was there, filling her to the brim and moving as only he could move. They might have been teenagers when they first learned this rhythm, but without anything to guide them besides desire and love, they'd discovered something special.

He stroked easily, as if they had forever to build this sensation into a spectacular mutual climax. But it wouldn't take forever. She could already feel tension coiling deep within her.

She looked into eyes darkened by passion. "We're good at this."

"Yeah, we are."

"Even after a layoff."

He chuckled. "A long layoff." As he held her gaze, his amused expression faded. Leaning down, he teased her mouth with soft, tender kisses. "Ready to bring it on home?"

"Yes, please."

"Me, too." Increasing the pace, he bore down until his powerful thrusts lifted her off the bed.

She hung on, gasping for breath as each contact took her higher.

"*Now*." He drove deep.

The momentum hurled her into the vortex. With a wild cry, she clung to him. He held her close and absorbed the impact, murmuring endearments and caressing her quivering body until his own climax took hold. Calling her name, he surrendered to his release.

His big body shuddered as she cradled him in her arms. She was humbled by how graciously he'd accepted her failings. His generosity of spirit had made it possible for them to have these last moments together. She was grateful.

But she'd miss the joy of holding him in the sweet aftermath of making love. Soon he'd rouse himself and want to cuddle and she cherished those times, too. Except he wasn't following his usual routine. Gradually his body settled over hers, pressing her into the mattress.

Wow, he was heavy. And her lungs were protesting. Enough of the tender cradling routine. She'd dealt with his dead weight after he'd passed out today. She wouldn't survive being smothered under him all night.

She tried shoving him away. Might as well try to move a house off its foundation and she was running out of breath. She didn't have enough to yell in his ear and shaking him had zero effect, so finally she pinched his butt.

He woke with a start and pushed up, bracing on his outstretched arms.

Like a swimmer emerging from a deep dive, she dragged in air.

"Good God, April!" He stared at her in horror. "I'm so sorry! I've never done that in my life. And to think I fell asleep on you, the woman I—" He halted his rant and a faint blush stained his rugged face. "Are you okay?"

"I am now." She reached up to stroke his stubbled chin. She wouldn't ask him what he'd started to say. She had a fair idea what it was. Better to leave it unspoken. "I would have nudged you earlier, but I kept thinking you'd move."

"Instead I almost crushed the life out of you. Unforgivable."

"Ryker, it's okay. I'm sure you're exhausted."

"That's no excuse." He eased away from her. "I'll be back in a sec."

After he left, she climbed out of bed and straightened the covers. She should send him back to his own bed for the rest of the night but she doubted he'd go.

When he came back in, she walked over and wound her arms around his neck. "You're too hard on yourself."

He drew her against his powerful chest. "It's just that I know how heavy I am, especially compared to you, and it's my responsibility to make sure I don't hurt you."

"Except that you were never going to hurt me. I'm a good pincher."

"You are." A brief smile appeared.

"And you're human, not some machine."

"I know. I've been forcefully reminded twice today."

"And humans need sleep. You would get more of that if you went back to your own room."

He frowned. "Is that what you want me to do?"

"No, but—"

"Then I'll stay, but I'll leave that fourth condom alone for now so I don't repeat that last stunt."

"Wise decision."

"But we're using it before we leave this house."

She gazed up at him. "Agreed. But we need sleep. If we do that spooning thing, we will sort of fit." She slipped out of his arms, walked back to the bed and switched off the bedside lamp. "Me, first." She climbed in and moved to the far side of the bed before turning her back to him. "Your turn."

The mattress sagged as he joined her and aligned his body with hers. "How's this?" He wrapped an arm around her waist and pulled her close.

"What's that I feel pressing against me?"

"Nothing." His breath was warm against her shoulder.

"I think it's something."

"Don't talk about it. You give that thing attention and we'll be back where we started."

She laughed. "Okay. I just realized we've never slept together before. I mean, we've *slept* together but we never went to sleep together."

"Didn't dare. Your folks or my mom would have come looking for us."

"Teenagers in love have it rough."

"All people in love have it rough."

"I suppose.' She closed her eyes and steadied her breathing. "Ryker, I can still feel—"

"I know. And I'm being so good about not fondling your breasts, too. Maybe it'll go down if I tell you about the guy at the bar."

"Okay."

"So…he overheard me tell the bartender I had a commuter airline business. And he wants to hire me to take him and his buddies fishing."

"That's fabulous. See, you walk into a bar, let people know what you do, and you get hired."

"That won't happen all the time, but he gave me a great idea. He thinks it's cool they'll be flying with a vet. So maybe that's a good angle. I'm gonna ask Mandy to put it on my website."

"You should." Although she'd rather not focus on his military career, others would gravitate toward him because of it. "It is a good angle."

"For most people, anyway." His voice held a trace of sadness.

"Absolutely. You should put pictures on the website of you in the cockpit of the—what did you fly again?"

"F-15 Eagle."

"Right. I should be able to remember that because of your tattoo."

"Except you don't want to think about fighter jets."

"No." She sighed. "I'm sorry, Ryker."

"It's fine." He gave her a squeeze. "Like you said, you were the girl with the anti-war bumper stickers plastered all over your locker. I can't expect you to change who you are, either." In the lengthening silence, his breath grew shallow and evened out. His arm relaxed. He was asleep.

But she lay in the darkness remembering those long-ago days. She'd been so intent on changing his mind about enlisting, so convinced she could do it. Meanwhile he'd carried her books and loaded them into the locker with all those pacifist slogans staring him in the face. He'd never mentioned them, never asked her to take them down.

He got points for that. On the other hand, he'd somehow believed she'd change her stance and accept his decision to head into battle. They'd both been delusional.

<u>15</u>

Ryker woke up before April and slipped out of bed without waking her. If he could manage it, he'd shower and shave, then slip back in beside her. He shaved first. Carefully. For a guy who passed out at the sight of blood, daily shaving with a blade was hazardous.

She'd left her dad's shaving cream on the counter yesterday so that helped. He'd tried an electric razor when he was in high school and hadn't liked it, so every morning since then he engaged in a ritual that could end with him taking a header. Bathrooms had a lot of hard surfaces.

Nobody in his family had acknowledged that shaving was a daily risk. Then again, he'd never reacted well to hovering so maybe they'd wisely decided to count on his steady hand and leave it at that. Now that he was back home he'd grow a beard. Not yet, though. He'd ride in the Labor Day Parade in his dress blues, which called for a close shave.

Stepping into the shower was a whole new experience after finding out about negative ions. He wouldn't mind an epiphany or two. April knew stuff. If she didn't know something she researched it.

Probably how she learned about hypnotherapy for her spider phobia.

Considering his daily shaving challenge, maybe he should give it a shot. What was the worst that could happen? He'd start clucking like a chicken or quacking like a duck. Okay, he'd try it, but he wouldn't tell anybody.

He dried off and walked back to her bedroom. April looked quite a bit like Snow White after the poisoned apple had put her in a trance. Except Snow White had worn clothes.

Without him crowding her, April had rolled onto her back and her tangled hair created dark waves on the pillow. Her heart-shaped face was completely relaxed, her brow smooth and peaceful. The room was warm so she hadn't bothered to pull up the sheet.

He couldn't help it. He wanted to look his fill. After this morning, he wouldn't be able to.

She wore t-shirts so much that her arms were tan up to the point where the sleeves stopped. The rest of her skin was Snow White pale except for some pink on her breasts. His beard had done that.

For someone so small, she had impressive curves. He lingered over her plump breasts, her narrow waist, the flare of her hips and the inviting triangle of dark hair at the juncture of her thighs. He memorized the shape of her calves and the delicacy of her ankles.

Her toenails were painted a soft blue-green. She was so beautiful that she made his eyes hurt. Either that or he'd gotten some soap in them during his shower because they were watering.

Slowly he approached the bed and dropped to one knee beside it. The fairytale had a scene like this, except for the clothes thing, of course. And he was no Prince Charming. But he leaned over her and kissed her lips, anyway. He'd always liked that part when Snow White's eyes fluttered open.

April sat straight up and banged her head against his.

He swore and so did she. He looked at her forehead and sure enough, she had a red spot that was already beginning to swell. "You need ice." He leaped up and took off out the door.

"Get the frozen peas in the freezer!" she called after him.

He returned with a bag of peas that likely had come from one of the veggie gardens out back. "Lie down."

"Did you bring one for yourself? You have a goose egg popping up, too."

"I'll be fine. Lie down and let me—"

"Give me that and go get another one." She took the peas and scooted to the far side of the bed. "We can lie here for a few minutes until the swelling goes down." She made a shooing motion with her hand. "Go get the other bag. Please. I don't want to have to explain this to my folks."

She had a point, so he made another trip and brought a second bag. Lying on their backs side by side, they barely fit on the bed. He laid the bag over his forehead. "That's not how it goes in the movies."

She chuckled. "Depends on the movie."

"You looked like Snow White."

"I looked like a goat?"

"No, Snow White, the princess, after she tasted the apple and fell asleep. Except you were naked, but otherwise you looked just like her."

"That's incredibly sweet. I'm sorry I didn't react like Snow White. I thought a bug was crawling on my mouth."

"A *bug*?"

"Well, yeah. I was sound asleep and had no idea you were there. Nobody's ever tried that before."

"I've never tried it before, either, and I sure as hell won't do it again."

"It might seem romantic, but when you're sound asleep and you feel light pressure on your mouth it could be anything. My first thought was a bug of some kind."

"Or a spider?"

"Yuck! Even worse! I don't freak out like I used to but jeez, can you imagine? I'll bet you'd freak out if you woke up and a big ol' spider was crawling over your mouth."

"It wasn't a spider. It was me."

"I know that *now*." She started to laugh.

"What?"

"Ryker."

"What, April?"

"I think we've found inner peas."

He groaned.

She elbowed him in the ribs. "Come on, admit it. That's funny."

"Okay, it's funny." He reached for her hand and slid his fingers through hers. "Listen, here's what

I'm thinking. We've worked through this situation and we've said everything that needs to be said."

"Except one more thing I thought of after you went to sleep."

"What's that?"

"I had all those slogans on my locker but you never objected. Even though you were gung-ho military, you didn't ask me to take them down."

"Why would I? That's what you believed."

She squeezed his hand. "I thought I was all about tolerance and you were way more tolerant than I was."

"But you had strong convictions. I might not have agreed with them, but I admired you for sticking by what you thought was right."

"That makes you a bigger person than me."

"I've always been bigger than you. I nearly squashed you last night."

"Be serious."

"All right, I'll be serious. Now you're being too hard on yourself. You were eighteen. Give yourself a break."

"You were the same age as me."

"Chronologically, but I was born old. Ask my brothers."

"I actually agree with that, but I need to say thank you for not asking me to take down my bumper stickers."

"You're welcome. I think we can take the peas off, now."

"Does that mean you're peas-ed off?"

He lifted the bag from his forehead and laid it on the nightstand. Then he raised up on one elbow to look at her. "You're too cute for your own good. That bag of peas is adorable, but it has to go." He picked it up and examined the spot where the lump had been. "Much better."

"You're getting bossy again."

"How's your tolerance for bossy people?"

"Normally not good, but I find your brand of bossiness somewhat arousing."

"Only somewhat?" He tossed the bag of peas over his shoulder and listened. They landed on the nightstand.

"More than somewhat."

"That's good news." He fondled her breast.

"Hey, your hand's cold!"

"Hang in there." He moved over her. "It won't be for long. And FYI, when you feel something on your mouth in a couple of seconds, it won't be a bug." He was glad they were teasing each other. Maybe then this last time wouldn't be so bittersweet.

But as he began loving her, as the magic began, he couldn't forget that once this was over, it would be the end. He drew out the process, but she was on fire for him.

After she triumphantly claimed one orgasm, he tried to slow things down, but she was so ripe and ready for another that he pumped faster, giving her what she clearly wanted. He paused once to lean over and brush his lips over hers. "Not a bug."

She dug her fingertips into his ass. "I know, silly."

"This is it. Last time."

"Then turn and burn, cowboy. Turn and burn."

The reference startled him. "That's from—"

"*Top Gun.*"

"But—"

She was breathing hard. "Watched it twenty times. Never got it."

That's when he knew it was hopeless. A person either related to that movie or they didn't. She didn't. But she'd asked him to turn and burn, so he did. They shared a noisy climax that nearly took his head off. And it was over.

He didn't lounge around in her bed afterward because the goats and chickens had to be fed. He considered the chore a good thing. What had been a lusty finale to their love affair could have turned into a mushy exchange of sentimental crap. They deserved better.

He offered to feed the critters while she took a shower and started breakfast. He'd miss the princesses and the Easter Eggers. Animals always seemed to know when someone was leaving and wouldn't be back. Others might argue with him but he believed it to be true.

While he helped April with breakfast she was friendly, but a subtle line had been drawn. He respected it. Once she'd left the bedroom she'd ceased to be his lover. That was fair. He didn't like it, but he agreed with the reasoning.

During breakfast on the porch, they stuck with safe topics—goats, chickens and vegetable gardens. His phone rang as they were finishing up. He'd left it on the kitchen counter so he excused himself and went to answer the call. The readout on the screen had a touch of inevitability.

After ending the call, he returned to the porch and sat beside her at the table. "That was the maintenance department at the airport. They have the part and expect to have my plane ready within the next hour."

She gazed at him, her expression calm. "Good timing."

"Guess so." Damn, this would be harder than he'd thought. He wanted to go back to being silly with bags of peas on their heads.

"I'll drop you off on my way over to Leigh's."

"I hate to leave without saying goodbye to your family." He wouldn't mind seeing little Pax again, either. She had a crazy name but she was cute as the devil.

"I'm sure they'll understand, but we can go there first, if you want. I'm not sure who will be up, but I could text my mom and—"

"No, never mind." God, he hated endings. "It's too much trouble just to pop in and say hello and goodbye. Besides, I need to get home. There's lots going on with Zane and Mandy's wedding. Zane asked if I'd fly them to their honeymoon resort as my wedding present, but we haven't worked out the details."

"What a cool idea. Are you going to paint *Just Married* on your plane?"

He smiled. "No."

"Hey, don't worry about my family. I'll tell them goodbye for you."

"That would be great. Thanks."

"Sure." Awareness flickered in her eyes for the first time since they'd left the bedroom. She looked away. "We should get going."

"Yep." He'd run out of safe conversational topics. She must have, too, because they worked silently together loading the dishwasher and tidying up the kitchen. He set the damp sponge in its holder on the sink. "What about your sheets? Did you want to throw them in the washing machine before we leave?"

"Already did, but thanks for reminding me. I'll pop them in the dryer and we can be off." She turned on the dishwasher. "Anything you need to gather up?"

Just her. "I'll go grab my bag of underwear. I left it in the bathroom."

"I was serious that you can have the other two pairs of peace symbol boxers."

"I'll take a pass." They weren't a gag gift for Badger anymore.

"Okay." She walked into the laundry room.

The air vibrated with all they weren't saying to each other. And it sucked. He walked down the hall to fetch the plastic bag he'd been using as a laundry hamper. He didn't glance into her bedroom.

Walking out of the house had a finality he didn't much enjoy, either. He carried her backpack and his plastic bag as he walked around to the driver's side of the Prius, opened the door and tucked her backpack behind her seat.

She paused by the hood. "Do you want to drive?"

"Nope. Just getting your door for you."

"Thank you." She came around to the side of the car and looked in. "You put the seat back like I had it."

"Of course."

She gazed up at him. "That's another reason I went out with you. You're nice." She cradled his jaw in her hand. "Do you think we could have one kiss goodbye without letting it get out of hand?"

His breath caught. "Absolutely."

"It feels wrong to just drive away from here without..."

"I know." He hooked the plastic bag on the door and pulled her close. "This has been special."

She nodded and her throat moved.

"It's not really goodbye, though." He slid his hand behind her neck and her ponytail brushed his skin. "We'll see each other around."

"But it'll be different, not like this."

Pain arrowed through his chest. "No, not like this." Leaning down, he fit his mouth gently to hers. So warm. He kept the pressure light and she did the same. She tasted of mint at first and then salt. He lifted his head and gazed into brown eyes filled with tears. His throat tightened. "We'll be okay." He sounded like he had a head cold.

She nodded again as tears dribbled down her cheeks.

He wiped them away with his thumbs. "We'd better go." He stepped back and she slid behind the wheel. Taking the plastic bag off the door, he closed it. When he came around to the passenger side, she'd pulled herself together enough to give him a watery smile. "We're off."

As time clicked away like the seconds on a doomsday clock, he finally spoke. "Look, I want to fix things between you and my family. What if I go back and tell everyone there's no hard feelings between us anymore?"

"And then what?"

"You can be friends with Mandy again. Mom can schedule massage appointments if she needs them. You could come out and go riding sometimes. You used to like that."

"I did." She sighed. "That would be nice. All of it sounds great. What about you and me, though?"

"We could take a shot at being friends. We've ironed out the issues, right?"

"I think so."

"I'm not saying we should meet at the Guzzling Grizzly for drinks. That's more like a date. But you could come out to the ranch without feeling weird."

"It would still feel weird the first time, but I'm sure that would fade. How much are you planning to tell them about us?"

He glanced at her. "The bare minimum to get the point across."

"Then nothing about—"

"I don't see why they have to know that we...had sex." He'd started to say *made love,* the term he'd been using most of the weekend. Might be time to switch to a more clinical word. "What are you planning to say to your folks?"

"Not much, but that doesn't mean our secret's safe. Leigh probably told John about giving me the condoms. My mom and dad aren't dumb. I'll bet they've drawn some conclusions. I can deal with them knowing. But your family...I can't explain it, but I'd rather they didn't."

"They won't hear it from me."

"Thank you."

He hesitated. "I wouldn't mind keeping in touch with your folks, too."

She greeted that with silence.

"Yeah, never mind. I can understand if you'd—"

"It's actually a great idea. They like you."

"And I like them. But if it makes you uncomfortable, forget it."

"I just had to adjust to the idea, but it's fine. More than fine. Text me and I'll send you their phone and email contacts."

"I don't have your number." Ludicrous.

"And I don't have yours. How crazy is that?"

"Easily fixed." He pulled his phone from his pocket. "Ready." Keying in the number she gave him, he texted her with *Here's to inner peas.* A muffled tune sounded from her backpack. "Done."

The exchange of numbers lightened his mood until the airport loomed dead ahead. Normally he got excited when he approached an airport, especially if his plane was parked there. "Are you sure you don't want me to fly up and get you when you're ready to come back?"

"I'm sure."

"See, I'm worried that now you're afraid to do it after what happened on the flight in. It's like being thrown from a horse. You have to get right back on."

"It has nothing to do with being afraid." She pulled up to the curb and turned to him. "If anything, I'd be more confident to fly with you after what happened. You were impressive."

"Just doing what I was trained to do."

"Like I said, impressive."

He liked it when she had that glow in her eyes, as if he was a hero. "Then let me fly up here and get you." He couldn't believe how the idea warmed his heart.

She shook her head. "That would send the wrong signal to both our families."

"Oh." *And you're sending the wrong signal to her, dumbass.* "You're right. Don't know what I was thinking."

"I do."

He hoped to hell she didn't.

"You can't help being nice. You wanted to save me the long drive."

Dodged a bullet. "It's a pilot thing. We don't drive if we can fly."

"I understand."

He picked up the plastic bag and opened his door. "Thanks for the ride."

"You bet."

He hesitated. "And thanks for...everything."

"Same to you, cowboy." She gave him that look again.

"Gotta go." He touched the brim of his hat and levered himself out of the car. "Say hello to your family for me."

"I will."

"Take care, now." He closed the door and watched her drive away. Damn. He missed her already.

_16_

A week later, April pulled into the drive of her little bungalow. It was good to be home. Although she loved spending time with her family, she'd become increasingly restless in Kalispell. She blamed it on being off work for so long.

She'd no sooner unpacked the rental car than her phone chimed with a text from Kendra McGavin. _Ryker thought you might be home by now. The Whine and Cheese Club would love to schedule a massage night at the ranch whenever you're free. Since there's five of us, we'd only ask for about twenty minutes each. Would that work for you?_

She gazed at the message. Ryker was fast. The fluttering sensation in her stomach was part anxiety and part excitement. He might not be around during this massage party. In fact, he likely wouldn't be. But he'd done what he'd promised. Clearly his mom, at least, was ready to give her another chance.

After exchanging a couple of texts with Kendra, she agreed to show up the next evening at seven with the portable massage table Geraldine had left along with a stack of cotton covers.

Geraldine used to take her show on the road quite often.

April hadn't nurtured that side of the business since hauling her stuff around wasn't her preferred method of working. She liked the cozy little space she rented in town from Dr. Merryville, the town's chiropractor.

But this setup would be a perfect icebreaker. She'd provide something of value while reestablishing a relationship with Kendra and her friends. It might even be fun.

Dating Ryker had been memorable for several reasons, and the Whine and Cheese Club had been one of them. They must have added a member, though. The original group had been Kendra and three girlfriends from her graduating class. And whoa, those ladies could party.

April and Ryker had come back from a trail ride one evening to find cars parked in front of the house and *Thriller* blaring from the sound system in the living room. Quickly ground-tying the horses, they'd crept up to the porch so they could peek in. Furniture had been moved, wine had been opened and *Thriller* moves had been happening. The memory still made her smile.

Maybe she ought to send one more text to Kendra. *PS, it's best if you don't drink wine before a massage.*

Kendra answered right back. *Don't worry. We'll save that for later.*

The following day was packed with appointments, and by six April wished she hadn't scheduled the Whine and Cheese ladies on her first day back. But she'd been eager to reconnect with Kendra and...oh, hell, she might as well admit that she was hoping to see Ryker.

With no time to fix a proper dinner, she ate a handful of frozen blueberries and another one of almonds. She took a quick shower to revitalize her flagging energy, loaded everything in her little pickup and set out for Wild Creek Ranch.

Turning off the main road onto the familiar dirt lane flooded her with memories. She'd loved it from her first visit until the last horrible one, when she'd driven out here to break up with him. The terrible things she'd said while standing in front of the house still haunted her.

Desperate to stop him from risking his life, she'd made wild accusations of selfishness and arrogance. She'd claimed that testosterone poisoning had given him an ego the size of Montana. She'd been especially proud of that insult.

He'd yelled, too, but only to protest that he wasn't any of those things. Which she knew now and had probably known then. He'd stammered because he'd been scared, scared of losing her.

She'd been scared, too. Terrified in fact. And he had been shot, so her fears hadn't been groundless. Still, she should never have threatened to leave him unless he gave up his dream. Because he was stronger than she'd expected, he hadn't caved.

Neither had she. The soldier and the pacifist. How could that ever work? Not in the real world. But that didn't keep her heart from pumping faster at the possibility of seeing him tonight.

And then she did. He appeared in her peripheral vision, galloping toward her across a meadow on a magnificent strawberry roan. The horse's mane whipped in the wind and Ryker leaned over its glossy neck, one hand anchoring his dark Stetson, the other grasping the reins.

He was on a collision course with her truck so she stepped on the brake, rolled down the windows and waited. He rode the way he made love, with confidence and enthusiasm. If he'd come to carry her off into the sunset on his mighty steed, she wasn't in the mood to resist. The Whine and Cheese ladies would be on their own.

But as he approached, he slowed the horse to a trot and finally to a walk. Rounding the front of her truck, he tipped his hat. The roan bobbed its head and showed off a dramatic white blaze.

She leaned out the window. "What's up?"

"I meant to be back before you arrived, but I went for a ride and ran across a mockingbird tangled in some baling twine. I guess they can get crosswise with that stuff just like the hawks and eagles."

"Is it okay?"

"It's fine. I unwound the twine and there was no significant damage. Gathered up the twine, too, which will make Zane happy. Anyway, glad I caught you."

"Why? Has the plan changed?"

"No, they're looking forward to it. But Mom said you'd brought a massage table. I'll help you get it inside."

She started to point out she'd loaded it by herself and could unload it by herself. Then she changed her mind. Independence was a virtue, but if a handsome cowboy offered to carry her massage table, she'd be a fool to reject his offer. "Thank you. That would be great."

"I'll meet you up at the house." He touched two fingers to the brim of his hat and reined his horse back onto the grass before setting off at an easy lope toward the ranch.

Mesmerized by the beauty of Ryker on a horse, an image she used to adore and hadn't seen in years, she sat unmoving until he glanced over his shoulder to see where she was. Oh, yeah. She was supposed to drive the truck. She took her foot off the brake and stepped on the gas.

She followed at a leisurely pace and enjoyed the view. Naturally he was riding on the grass instead of on the road. He didn't want to stir up clouds of dust she'd have to drive through. That was so Ryker.

The house and the barn came into view and everything looked much the same, although the roof on the house was now green galvanized tin. Many people in the area had reroofed to help protect against fire. But the single-story log home had the same footprint she remembered. Chairs on the front porch still invited visitors to stop and sit a spell. Yellow and orange chrysanthemums bloomed in the beds on either side of the porch steps.

She parked at the end of a row of vehicles and Ryker rode up beside her truck and dismounted.

He dropped the reins, ground-tying his horse the way they had years ago when they'd spied on the Whine and Cheese ladies. He managed to get to her door and open it before she snapped out of her daze. The week they'd been apart seemed like a month. Except for texting him the phone numbers and email addresses for her family, she hadn't communicated with him.

He held out a hand, a totally unnecessary gesture, but she took it because she wanted an excuse to touch him. His hand was warm and strong, exactly how it had been when he'd stroked her naked body.

She gulped. "Any problems with your plane on the way home?"

"Not a one. Smooth as silk." He let go of her hand. "How was the drive?"

"Fine. Have you heard from the guy you met at the bar?"

"I did just today. We're set up for next week. If I fly up early in the morning, I'll have time to go see Leigh and Pax if they're okay with it. Maybe I'll catch John or your mom and dad there, too."

"That would be wonderful." His eagerness to see her family touched her. "Listen, thanks for talking to your mom. This group massage is perfect. Less pressure than if your mom had booked a private appointment."

"She came up with it after I talked to her. This way her friends can see that we're friends again, too. You probably don't need extra business, but you should get some, anyway."

"I'm happy to grow the business. If I get to the point I can't handle it, I'll see about hiring someone to help with the client load. More massage therapy is always a good thing."

"I thought you'd like the plan." His stance was casual, but his gaze was warm.

Dangerous though it might be, she basked in that warmth. "Definitely. Who's the fifth member of the club? I only remember Deidre, Judy and Christine."

"Aunt Jo."

"Oh. That makes sense. But why wasn't she a member before?"

"They invited her, but her husband didn't approve. They're divorced, now."

"As well they should be. What a medieval attitude. It'll be good to see her, too." The easy flow of conversation was at odds with the fluttering in her stomach. His voice stroked her nerve endings to create a delicious vibration.

"Oh, and I think Deidre was married when you last saw these ladies."

"They all were except your mom."

"Well, Deidre got a divorce about five years ago, but Christine and Judy are still married. Don't know if any of that matters."

"It's nice to have the background." Especially delivered in his deep baritone. "Thanks."

"I can tell you they're all super excited about the massage party. We should get in there. Where's the table?"

"In the back of the truck. It has a carrying case. If you'll get that I'll take in the satchel with all my supplies."

"You don't have your backpack?"

"It doesn't hold all the things I like to have for something like this."

"Is it heavy?"

She smiled. What a sweetie. "I can handle it." Walking around to the passenger side, she took out her bag of tricks.

Ryker lifted the case out of the back as if it weighed nothing and hoisted it to his shoulder. He'd chosen the uninjured one, though. "Let's roll."

She walked beside him as they skirted the parked cars and headed for the path leading to the house. "How's your shoulder?"

"Better, thanks. I've established an exercise routine that's helping."

She looked over at him. "So would massage."

"I know." He gave her a brief smile. "I'm not there yet."

His smile followed by a loaded comment seriously jacked up her heart rate. She took a calming breath. "I suppose I'm not, either. I just hate that I could do you some good and yet..." She sighed. "I'll be honest. I've missed you."

"Same here." He gave her a quick glance. "We need to give it time."

"Yep." She walked a little faster so she could go ahead of him up the narrow path to the front porch. Laughter spilled out the open window, but no music. "I guess they're not dancing to *Thriller* tonight."

"Mom's taking a break from her eighties tunes. It's Turkish music these days."

"How come?"

"Their new thing. Belly dancing."

"Now *that* sounds like fun."

"They like it. Deidre came up with an idea for the Labor Day Parade and they're going for it."

"They'll be belly dancing in the parade?" She climbed the porch steps.

"That's what I hear."

"Awesome." Crossing the porch, she tapped on the door.

Kendra threw it open. "You're here!" She glanced over April's shoulder. "Good job, son. We'd like it set up in the middle of the living room, please."

"Are you sure?" April had never worked that way. "Wouldn't you rather create a quiet retreat somewhere else in the house?"

"We could, I suppose." Kendra didn't look excited about the concept. "Is that what you'd rather have?"

"Not at all. You're the client. I just—"

"Good then. We like the idea of massage-in-the-round."

"Like theater-in-the-round?"

"Exactly."

April glanced back at Ryker, who stood patiently with the carrying case balanced on his shoulder. "Looks like it goes in the middle of the room."

"Where the coffee table is normally," Kendra added. "We've already moved the furniture back."

"I'm on it." He lowered his burden and proceeded to take out the table and set it up in no time flat. "There you go."

April stared at him. "You set it up way faster than I could."

"Piece of cake." He grinned. "After you've field stripped an M16, anything else is—"

"Ryker McGavin!"

"Oops." Looking like a kid caught with matches, he turned to face his mother.

Kendra glared at him, her hands planted on her hips. "I distinctly remember you telling me that as a pilot you wouldn't be dealing with rifles and maybe not even hand guns."

"Well, um, things changed. In my squadron, at least."

"And you somehow failed to inform me of this?"

"Yes, ma'am. I knew you wouldn't like it."

"You were right." She walked over and hugged him. "So it's probably better that I didn't know." Then she stepped back and gazed at him as if she'd never seen a more beautiful sight than her eldest son standing in her living room alive and well. "Okay, soldier." Her voice was shaky. "You're dismissed. We ladies will be disrobing and you don't need to be around for that."

"That's for sure. I'm outta here." He glanced at April. "But text me when you're ready to pack up. I'll stow this back in your truck."

"I can do it. I don't want to be any extra trouble." But she was dying to find out if his mother knew about the bullet wound. Didn't sound like it.

"No trouble. I'll just be up in the old log cabin on the hill. That's where I'm bunking for now."

"Nice!" She'd always been intrigued by the historic cabin, the first structure built on the land by the original homesteaders. Last she remembered Kendra had used it for storage but it must have been repurposed. "Okay, I'll text you when we're all done, here."

"Unless we ply her with wine and teach her some belly dancing moves." Deidre, a plump woman who used to be a brunette and was now a redhead, gave her a wink. "Once you get involved with the Whine and Cheese Club, you never know what might happen."

Ryker looked at April and smiled. "If you need rescuing, let me know."

"Thanks, cowboy." Was he *flirting* with her? Then again, she could be imagining that twinkle in his eyes because she wanted to see it there.

He left, taking the fizzy sensation of sensual overload with him. She'd have to work harder at this friendship thing. So far she sucked at it.

Since the Whine and Cheese ladies had witnessed that exchange, they were probably as confused about the relationship as she was. She glanced around the room. "Hey, it's great to see you all again. Everybody looks fabulous."

"Thanks," Deidre said. "You, too. It's been a while. Do you remember all our names?"

"Absolutely. Deidre, Christine and Judy." Christine was a good six inches taller than Judy. She was still a blond and Judy was still a brunette. That left a slender woman with short gray hair and large hoop earrings. "And Jo."

"I wasn't part of the club when you lived here before."

"No, but I saw you plenty of times around the ranch. How's Mandy?"

"Great. She said to tell you hello. She plans to book a massage soon."

"Terrific. It'll be great to see her." It was coming together the way Ryker had said it would if he paved the way. All she had to do was maintain an easy friendship with him and these lovely people would be her friends again, too.

"I'm amazed that you remember after all this time," Christine said.

"Are you kidding? Ten years ago, when I peeked in that window over there and saw women my mom's age rocking out to Michael Jackson, it made an impression."

Kendra laughed. "You ain't seen nothin' yet, girl."

"We should give her a demonstration." Judy rotated her hips. "We're damn good, if I do say so."

"I definitely want a demonstration after we're done."

"Then let's get this massage program in gear," Kendra said. "Do you need any help setting up?"

"I brought my diffuser, so that requires an outlet and some water."

"I'll take care of that. I just bought one for myself."

April took it out of the satchel and handed it to her. "What scent does everybody want?"

Kendra turned to the group. "How about one scent for all of us to make it less complicated?"

"Cinnamon!" Deidre called out.

"But I like sweet orange better," Judy said.

"Clove!" Christine waved a hand in the air.

"Hang on." April dug in her bag and took out all three. "We can mix these and it'll be fine." She glanced at Kendra and Jo. "You two good with that?"

They both nodded.

"Then here you go." After handing the bottles to Kendra, she pulled out a fitted cover for the table and another for the face cradle. She'd brought sheets for the sake of modesty, although the lights and the number of people made this session more like massage school than a client appointment.

The soft hiss of the diffuser told her Kendra had that organized so she pulled out her large bottle of massage oil. "I'm ready. Who wants to be first?"

"Me!" Christine kicked off her shoes. Then she whipped off her shirt, her capris, and finally her bra before climbing onto the table and lying face down. "All set!"

"Do you want a sheet?"

"Nah, what's the point?" She settled into the face cradle. "They've seen it all, anyway."

April was startled but charmed by Christine's unselfconscious behavior. The massage-in-the-round made sense to her, now. These women were totally comfortable with each other and enjoyed sharing experiences like this one. While she gave Christine her massage, the others sorted through a large canvas bag and stripped down so they could try on and evaluate their belly dancing costumes.

After Christine's twenty minutes, she switched with Judy, who also flung off her clothes with abandon while April quickly changed the table cover. Gold coins jingled and conversation hummed as the women fooled with their costumes.

"Mandy did an awesome job, Jo," Deidre said. "I can't believe she found the time to make this stuff when she's also sewing her wedding dress *and* her bridesmaid dresses. Be sure and tell her she's incredible."

"I tell her all the time, but I'll tell her you made a point of it tonight. I don't know where she got this talent. I can't sew a lick."

Kendra groaned. "Me, either. Hey, Deidre, you need to drape a scarf over your chest, girlfriend. You have too much boobage going on."

"I beg your pardon, Kendra, dear. I need all this boobage. I want Jim's eyes to fall out of his head when we dance down Main Street."

"Oooo, she said Jim's name!" Judy lifted her head from the face cradle. "Rhyming game!"

"Me, first!" Christine began a chant. "Jim and Deidre sittin' in a tree, doin' things we *never* wanna see! Take it, Kendra!"

"Jim and Deidre sittin' in a bush, she leans over and grabs his tush! Take it, Jo!"

"Jim and Deidre sittin' in a truck, first they kiss and then they —"

"Omigod, Jo!" Kendra hooted with laughter. "You're gonna shock poor April."

"She's fine with it." Judy's voice was muffled by the face cradle. "I just heard her snort."

April got the giggles so bad she had to take a break from Judy's massage.

"Yay!" Christine wiggled her hips and coins jingled. "We cracked her up!"

April finally got a grip, cleared her throat and went back to the massage. "Who's Jim?"

"Faith's dad," Kendra said. "We hired her last spring and now he works with us, too."

"Which is not the pertinent info," Deidre said. "What you need to know, April, is that Jim Underwood is my sweet love bucket, the honey in my tea, the sugar in my coffee, the—"

The other four made gagging sounds.

"Don't mind them. They're just pea-green with envy."

"After all this I can't wait to meet him."

"I'll be sure to introduce you after the parade," Deidre said. "Will you have an entry?"

"Maybe. Still hatching the idea. I'd like to, though. Geraldine always had some sort of wacky float."

"That's for sure," Kendra said. "Like the motorized massage table that tipped over and the giant bottle of massage oil that sprung a leak. Geraldine didn't have a talent for parade floats."

April smiled. "But she was great for comic relief."

"We're handling the comic relief this year," Jo said. "The Whine and Cheese and Belly Dancing Club."

"I hope you all appreciate the sacrifice I'm making to participate," Kendra said. "Normally I'd be with my boys representing Wild Creek Ranch, but I know how desperately you need my dancing skills. And don't you dare laugh, Deidre Wiggins! I'll be amazing by then."

"You'll all be awesome." April finished Judy's massage and changed the cover so that Deidre could climb on. "I can't wait to see this. I have fond memories of that parade." Especially Ryker looking like a god and carrying a Wild Creek Ranch flag as he rode by on a high-stepping horse. "Do you still have the ranch flag, Kendra?"

"We do. Zane's been carrying it since Ryker's been gone. He'll do it again this year, too, because Ryker's been asked to carry an American flag and wear his dress blues."

April's chest tightened.

"He'll look great doing that," Christine said. "I'm almost sorry I'll be in the parade and can't watch him ride by, so straight and proud."

"I'll get Jim to shoot a video of the Wild Creek entry." Deidre settled face down on the table. "He'll be there anyway to get footage of us and we need a video of our favorite vet all decked out in his soldier duds."

April poured oil into her palm in preparation for beginning Deidre's massage. She'd better add a comment, and soon, if she wanted Ryker's family and friends to continue being friendly.

"A video's a good idea. I'm sure he'll look absolutely wonderful." There, she'd said something positive even if her words had sounded a little gravelly.

It wasn't a lie, either. Kendra would love having that video and Ryker would look brave and handsome in his dress blues. But the uniform represented all the reasons why she could never be with him. She didn't want to see him wearing it.

<u>17</u>

Ryker sighed. He should have planned better. His offer to reload the massage table for April had left him at loose ends, and he wasn't good with loose ends. He wasn't the type to pick up a book to fill the time and he'd decided against having a TV in the cabin. He wasn't into sitting in front of a screen, anyway. Inactivity drove him nuts.

He couldn't hang out with his brothers because they had stuff going on. He saw Cody and Faith all the time during the day but at night they disappeared into their little hideaway in the trees. Same thing with Zane and Mandy. They were around in daylight hours but at night they were tucked away in their own cozy home adjacent to the ranch.

That was as it should be. If jealousy pricked him because they'd been lucky enough to find a person to spend the rest of their days with, he'd get over it.

That left the twins, Bryce and Trevor. Trevor was out of town taking special training so he'd be better equipped to fight the forest fires that were becoming an increasing problem in the area. Bryce recently had been hired to manage the Guzzling

Grizzly so he'd be working. Ryker had an important subject to discuss with him, so he'd planned to head into town some night soon and help him close the bar. That way they could talk uninterrupted.

But that plan didn't satisfy his current need for meaningful activity. Might as well get into his exercise routine. Repetitive exercise bored him to tears, but it helped with his shoulder so he launched into it. And then did another round. And another.

When April's text came through, he grabbed the phone like a man sinking through the hole in a frozen lake. He texted back that he'd be right there, tucked his phone in his pocket, put on his hat and left the cabin. All the vehicles were still parked in front of the house and the exotic sound of Turkish music increased in volume the closer he came.

April sat in one of the porch chairs waiting for him. Her carrying case for the massage table sat next to her, along with her satchel containing all her supplies.

He climbed the steps. "So they didn't lure you into their belly dancing routine?"

"No." She smiled. "I watched them perform, which was fun. They tried to get me to try it, but I begged off, so they helped me pack up. I promised to come back sometime soon when I wasn't recovering from a trip and a full day at work."

"Was the massage session a success?" He leaned against the porch railing and gazed at her.

"It was. They're a riot." She pushed out of the chair. "But I'm ready to go home. And despite being able to carry that table by myself, I'd appreciate your help."

"Absolutely. That was the plan. Let me take your satchel, too." He hoisted the table to his left shoulder and grabbed the satchel in his other hand.

"Thank you." She went ahead of him down the walkway to the parking area. "I can't remember the last time I've been this exhausted."

Alarm bells rang in his head. She hadn't had much rest during their weekend together, either, but she hadn't complained about it. "I'm going to follow you home, make sure you get there okay."

"Oh, Ryker, no. I'm on the other side of town. That's silly. I'll be fine."

"It's not silly. Tired people run off the road. The very fact that I'm behind you will help you stay alert, but if you should have a problem, you won't be out there alone."

"I can't let you do that."

"Sure you can. Let me give you an excellent reason so you won't feel guilty about it. I've been wanting to stop by the Guzzling Grizzly and talk with Bryce about something. If I follow you home, I can come back by way of the bar."

"I'm not buying it. You don't need to stop by the Guzzling Grizzly. You could just call him on the phone."

"Not about this. It requires seeing him in person."

"Oh. All right, then. Thank you. Just follow me that far. I can certainly make it from there. It's only a couple of miles more and I promise not to crash."

He heaved a sigh. "I want to see you safely to your door."

"This is starting to sound like that night in my folks' backyard. Are you guarding me again?"

"Maybe. Do you really hate it so much?"

"No." Her answer was soft. "I guess not."

"Good." He'd reached her little white truck so he loaded her table in the back and carried her satchel around to the passenger seat. She'd already climbed behind the wheel by the time he accomplished that but she'd left the door open. He walked around the front bumper and over to her door. "I have to run up to the cabin and come back with my truck. Promise you won't leave."

"I won't." She gazed up at him. "Does your mom know about your bullet wound?"

"No."

"I didn't think so from the way she reacted when you mentioned the M16."

"Yeah, that was a dumb slipup on my part. But she has no reason to know about it unless I tell her. I haven't had my shirt off when she's been around."

"How about your brothers? Do they know?"

"They do, but we all decided there was no point in making a big announcement to Mom. Then after the way you freaked out, I was even more sure I should wait. She'll find out eventually, but the longer I've been home, the less it will matter. At least that's my theory."

She nodded. "Sounds reasonable."

"Hope so." He moved away from her truck. "I won't be long." He jogged up to the cabin. The keys were under the driver's seat so he was on his way in no time.

She'd backed out and sat with the engine idling. When he flicked his lights, she put the truck in gear and started down the ranch road.

If she hadn't wanted him to follow her he would have risked making her mad by doing it anyway. It wasn't like she could have stopped him. But she'd given in, maybe because she was too tired to argue. In any case, she wasn't acting like her usual feisty self.

She drove under the speed limit the whole way. He had to keep easing off the gas so he wouldn't run up her back end. At last she pulled into the driveway of a small bungalow in a well-kept neighborhood. He hadn't done this as some sneaky way to find out where she lived, but now he knew. He parked behind her, got out and walked up to where she stood beside her truck.

"Thank you, Ryker." She sounded subdued. "I'm glad you did that because I stayed more alert with you back there. I kept checking my mirror to make sure I could see your lights. But you're free to go. I'm here."

"I'll carry your table in."

"You can leave it. I'll bring it in tomorrow."

"Why? I'm right here." He hauled the table out of the back and opened her passenger door to get the satchel.

She stood and watched him. "You sure are persistent, cowboy."

"I just believe in finishing what I start." He mounted the steps to the bungalow's small porch and waited for her to unlock the front door and turn on some lights. Then he carried both things into her living room. It had a cozy feel with a sofa, two chairs and a braided rug on the floor, but the furniture was more April sized than made for someone who was six-four. "Where do you want these?"

"You can leave them right there."

He gazed at her. "Hey."

"In the spare bedroom. I use it as an office. I'll show you." She walked ahead of him down a short hall and turned on the overhead. "Over in that corner would be great. Thanks."

He set them down and noticed the bookshelf with her debate trophies lined up on it. He gestured to them. "Nice."

"Thanks. I..." She began to weave.

He crossed the room in two strides and caught her before she fell. "Good God, you're burning up!"

"I just need some rest."

"No kidding." Scooping her up, he carried her to the next door down, figuring that would be her bedroom. Bingo. He laid her on the bed and went in search of aspirin and water. When he returned, she hadn't moved and her eyes were closed.

He sat on the edge of the bed and supported her while he coaxed her into taking two aspirin.

"That's fine," she mumbled, looking at him with eyes that were too bright. "Go see Bryce."

"Not yet." He left her only long enough to fill a bowl with cool water and grab a washcloth from her bathroom.

She made a small sound of protest when he started taking off her clothes.

"Hush. We need to get that fever down." He'd helped his mom do this for Cody one night. As he gently wiped her hot skin with the cool cloth, she closed her eyes and her breathing evened out.

He lost track of how long he sat on the edge of the bed while he stroked the washcloth over her face and body. Eventually her skin cooled enough that he decided to quit doing it so she could sleep. After gently working her under the covers, he rested his hand on her forehead. Much better. He turned off the light and left the room.

Now what? He checked the time on his phone. Because it was a weeknight, Bryce would be closing the bar in about fifteen minutes. Walking into April's tidy kitchen, he evaluated the contents of her refrigerator. She had a few fresh veggies that likely had come from her folks' garden and a small bowl of colored eggs. She had some frozen blueberries in the freezer along with a carton of ice cream.

The veggies were nutritious but not what he considered sick bay food. She needed a big kettle of homemade soup that could be heated up as needed and he knew exactly where to get it. Picking up the keys she'd left on the coffee table, he locked her in and drove to the Guzzling Grizzly.

Great timing. The place had cleared out and Bryce had the keys in his hand ready to lock the front door. He grinned. "Sorry, mister. Bar's closed."

"No worries. I know the manager. He promised me a drink on the house anytime I got thirsty."

"You thirsty, big brother?" Bryce might not consider himself a musician anymore but he still looked like one with hair almost to his collar. Combined with the Stetson and yoked shirt with silver piping he'd chosen to wear tonight, he looked like he could have taken the stage at the Country Music Awards.

"I'm mighty thirsty if it's free. And if you'll join me."

"Can't hardly resist an offer like that. It's not every day a saddle tramp comes along who's willing to help me drink up the profits." Bryce moved behind the bar and took two glass mugs from the glittering pyramid behind the bar. They'd all gone through the dishwasher in back, but Bryce insisted they be hand-polished until the facets around the base threw off rainbows.

"You could give me a bottle and save yourself some trouble."

"That's not how I treat family." He drew two perfect mugs of beer and set them on the gleaming bar. Then he came around to take a stool next to Ryker. "What brings you out tonight?"

"April gave massages to the Whine and Cheese Club and—"

"I heard that was going down. Don't tell me. You lined up with the ladies and got yourself a massage. Now you have to drink beer with your brother so you can top off your testosterone level."

"Nice try. I helped her carry in her massage table, and then—"

"Color me surprised."

"Do you want to hear this or not?"

He laughed. "Just giving you a hard time. We all know the story isn't over when it comes to you and April."

"Yeah, it is." He took a sip of his beer. "Except for this one thing."

"Uh-huh."

Ryker filled him in on April's collapse and made his request for a big pot of the soup that was a staple at the Guzzling Grizzly. "I'm hoping you've got some back there and a pot I can borrow. I'll pay for it."

"Damn straight you will. A couple of beers won't be missed but two gallons of our signature soup is a whole other level of skimming."

"I know that. But it's perfect for the situation and she's got nothing that's easy to fix. I checked."

"But you're just friends, now, right?"

"Right."

Bryce's smirk said it all.

"Like I've already said, we had a chance to iron things out in Kalispell and we're too different to ever get along."

"Then maybe I should take her the soup. I was never a soldier boy. Never wanted to be one."

Ryker glared at him.

"Ha! You flat-out failed that test, big brother! Good luck selling this *we're just friends* crap. You know damned well I'd never date your ex, but some joker will, and I fear for his safety."

He hadn't thought of that. In a town the size of Eagles Nest, he'd likely hear if April started seeing someone, especially if it got serious. Now that he'd smoothed the way for her to reconnect with his family, he'd definitely hear about it. If she *married* the jerk, he might be invited to the damned wedding. Terrific.

"I can see that's a new concept for you."

"It is." He drank more beer. "Most of the time I love living in a small town, but..."

"Tell me about it. Try being me standing at the altar when the maid of honor comes in to tell me the bride's left. There's not a soul in Eagles Nest who doesn't know that story. It was one of the main reasons I spent all those months with Trevor wrangling cattle for that rich dude in Texas. Nobody down there knows. It was heaven."

"I'm sorry I wasn't here for you, buddy."

"I'm glad you weren't. It was miserable."

Ryker glanced over at him. "Since we're on the subject, I've been wanting to ask you something."

"What?" Bryce took a mouthful of beer.

"I want you to play guitar for Zane and Mandy's wedding."

His brother spewed his beer.

Ryker flinched because Bryce had always been a champion spitter and the beer reached the pyramid of mugs. "Damn, I'm sorry. I shouldn't have said that when you had a mouthful."

Bryce ignored the beer dripping everywhere and gazed at him. "You want me to play for Zane and Mandy's wedding?"

"Yes."

"This is August. The wedding's next month. I haven't touched my guitar since last October. Even if I wanted to play for them, which I regret to say I don't, I'm so rusty that I'd be an embarrassment."

"You have time to get in shape. The wedding's not until the last weekend of September. Zane was reluctant to ask so I said I would."

"Zane is reluctant because he witnessed my humiliation. My music is all tangled up with memories of that terrible day and honestly, it's a wonder I still have my guitar since whenever I look at it I think of Charity."

"She should be arrested by the name police. Charity, my ass."

"Yeah, I even wrote her a song about selfless giving." Bryce took a swallow of his beer. "I hate saying no to Zane but I wouldn't be an asset to his wedding. I'm sort of surprised he still wants me to play."

"All I can relay is the intel I've gathered since I've been back. It seems that ever since you turned pro with that guitar, Zane has envisioned you playing for his wedding, no matter where it took place or who he was marrying. Cody has the same fixation, but he's willing to let it go. Not Zane. He has his heart set on your guitar music being sprinkled liberally throughout his nuptials."

"I hate that he's so attached to the idea, but I could easily ruin his wedding and I refuse to take that chance."

"Are you willing to at least think about it?"

"No. I'd rather have someone drive toothpicks under my fingernails."

"Okay, I'll tell Zane."

Bryce frowned. "Can you soften it?"

"How would you suggest I do that? How about *Bryce would rather have someone squeeze Play-doh under his fingernails*? Would that work for you?"

"I'll get your soup."

"I'll help you clean up."

April was still asleep when Ryker let himself back into her house. He crept into her bedroom and felt her forehead. Normal. Fevers could be like that, spiking quickly and then dropping just as fast when action was taken. He was glad he'd been there to take that action.

He put the kettle of soup in her refrigerator and left a note explaining where it had come from and that he'd put her keys under the third rock to the left of her front walkway counting from the porch. He'd considered leaving them in the house but then he wouldn't have been able to lock the deadbolt.

Driving away was difficult but he'd have trouble explaining why he'd spent the rest of the night at her house. She was sick, but she wasn't at death's door. He'd text her in the morning, though. Just to make sure she got the note and the soup.

_18_

Sidelined. April dragged through the next few days eating soup and reclaiming her energy. She'd burned the candle at both ends and now she was paying for it. If not for Ryker and the magic soup he'd brought, she might have ended up paying more dearly.

She'd texted to thank him and he'd texted back with a smiley face. She'd decided to let it go at that and she hadn't heard from him again. Although he'd undressed her and given her a sponge bath the night of the massage party, now he was leaving her alone.

That was good, right? Casual friends didn't keep in constant contact.

Mandy booked a massage and hand-delivered a wedding invitation when she arrived. The massage session was chatty as they caught up with each other's lives. Mandy talked about the McGavins, including Ryker, without awkwardness or hesitation, so it appeared that everyone was on the same page.

Because Labor Day was fast approaching, April spent all her spare time on her parade entry.

She needed every extra minute, too, especially because she wanted to keep her idea a secret until the day of the parade. That meant waiting until the night before to assemble everything she'd gathered for the mini-float she'd pull with a rented ATV.

She had the folks at Home Depot in Bozeman to thank for the structure, a rectangular box on wheels that was sturdy enough to support her portable massage table. She'd borrowed a CPR training mannequin from the hospital and one of the nurses had loaned her a wig for it. Covered with a sheet, the mannequin looked like an extremely pale and passive client lying on her table.

She'd found a twenty-cubic-foot bag of green recycled peanuts online. Transferring those little suckers into smaller plastic bags had taken freaking forever. But when she tucked them around the base of the massage table, they looked close enough to what she had in mind, especially from a distance.

She was up early the morning of the parade because everyone had to rendezvous in the Eagles Nest Diner parking lot at seven sharp. Time for the finishing touch to her float. She taped a cardboard sign to each side of the massage table.

Done. She stood back and smiled. Ryker might, too, if he happened to see her float and read the sign—FIND YOUR INNER PEAS WITH APRIL HARRIS. Below that she'd added her website and phone number.

The parking lot was a madhouse. April left her float and got into the line of people waiting for their assigned parade position.

"April!" Kendra's voice carried over the noise of the crowd.

She turned as the Whine and Cheese Club hurried over in a swirl of brightly colored chiffon, their gold coins and bangles jingling. "Hey!" April swept an arm to encompass all of them. "You look fabulous, ladies!"

"Don't we, though?" Deidre executed a hip rotation. Her boobage was on full display.

"We had a slight change of plans for our entry." Kendra made a face. "Everyone was worried that I'd hurt my leg if I danced the entire parade route, so we'll be doing our number on a horse-drawn wagon, instead."

"Good." April nodded. "I wondered about that."

"It was a battle to convince her," Jo said. "She's one stubborn dudette. But we won."

"And guess who's driving that wagon?" Deidre winked at April.

"Jim?"

"None other." She motioned to a tall, lanky cowboy standing a short distance away, thumbs hooked in his belt loops. He looked highly amused by the goings-on. "Come over and meet April, Jim. April Harris, this is Jim Underwood."

He touched the brim of his hat. "Pleased to meet you, ma'am."

"I'm pleased to meet you, too, Jim." *I've heard so much about you.*

"Oh, April." Jo clapped her hand to her head. "I meant to say something about your adorable float first thing. Great idea!"

"Thank you."

"It's so clever," Christine said. "And it even looks disaster proof."

"I hope so. What number are you guys?"

Jim help up a plastic square. "Five."

Kendra glanced at the registration table. "Your turn. Maybe you'll be close to us."

"That would be awesome." She stepped over to the table, signed in and was given her number. "I'm six! Right behind you!"

"Perfect." Kendra gave her arm a squeeze. "I heard you were under the weather for a while. Are you feeling better?"

"Much better." She almost added *thanks to Ryker* but decided against it. "I just let myself get run down. I'm fine, now."

"Glad to hear it," Judy said. "We loved that session with you. We've talked about making it a monthly event if you can put up with us that often."

"Are you kidding? That would be a blast. I promise to be more rested up for the next one."

"Excellent." Judy gave her a thumbs-up.

"Time to get in line," Jim said. "Head for the wagon, ladies."

"Can't wait to see the show!" April called after them.

"Hello, April."

She glanced up at the sound of the deep baritone she knew so well. Ryker sat astride the same strawberry roan he'd ridden the night she'd come out to the ranch. But this was a different Ryker. The Stetson had been replaced by a dark blue triangular cap and dark aviator shades. Instead of a t-shirt, jeans and boots, he wore what his mom had referred to as dress blues.

Now she knew what that was—light blue dress shirt, black tie, dark blue jacket and pants, polished black oxfords. He'd transformed from the cowboy she knew into a handsome stranger. The jacket had stuff on it, lots of stuff. The emblem on the sleeve of his jacket was a chevron. She knew that much. The pin with wings probably indicated he was a pilot. Other badges and pins were a mystery, but a couple of them looked like medals.

His expression was hard to read, especially since he was wearing dark glasses. "What do you think?"

"I don't know what to think. You're...different."

"Not really."

"It's like I don't know you when you're dressed like this."

"But I'm the same guy."

"Number six! We need number six, pronto!"

"I have to go." She held up her number as if that would prove it.

"Me, too. Your float's amazing." He wheeled his horse and trotted away.

She dashed over to her ATV where an older woman stood tapping her clipboard with a pen. "I'm so sorry, ma'am. I'm here."

The woman, who was decked out in a fringed jacket and fringed leather pants, looked at her and smiled. "April Harris, you haven't changed a bit. Still stuck on Ryker McGavin."

She knew that smoker's voice. "Ellie Mae Stockton! How have I missed seeing you since I got back?" The eighty-something woman had been a clerk at Pills and Pop forever.

"Beats me, honey."

"I'll bet I know." She climbed on the ATV and started the engine. "You work days and I only shop at night."

"That must be it. Great float, by the way."

"Thanks, Ellie Mae."

"Get moving, now. You're right behind the Whine and Cheese Club."

"I know." She pulled up behind the tailgate and waved at the Whine and Cheese ladies. Now she wished she'd asked Ryker which number he had. As she waited in line, Deidre came to the back of the wagon and called to her. "Did you see Ryker in his dress blues?"

"I did just now."

"Doesn't he look gorgeous?"

"Um, yes. He does." She hadn't expected to like seeing him in uniform. "What number are the McGavin brothers?"

"Number one! Ryker's leading the parade!"

"Oh." Of course he was. And her traitorous heart swelled with pride. "Who's taking a video since Jim's driving your wagon?" She couldn't see Ryker from her position back here, but she might get a peek at someone's video later.

"Mandy volunteered," Deidre said. "Okay, we're moving out! See you up at the park!"

"Right!" She'd forgotten that everyone gathered there after the parade for the speeches.

Turkish music blared from the wagon as it rumbled out of the parking lot. The Whine and Cheese ladies received a wildly enthusiastic response from the crowd packing the sidewalks along Main Street. Everybody clapped and cheered for April's float, too, which gratified her.

She waved to people she knew and some she didn't. Mandy called out from behind her camcorder and a couple of high school buddies yelled her name, too. She'd texted with them since moving back but hadn't found time for a girls' night out. She'd fix that. Work was important but she'd been driving herself too hard. She—

"Runaway!" The panicked screech came from the back of the parade.

April put on the brakes and turned. A horse without a rider barreled down the street as people scattered.

"Everybody down!" Jim yelled as he steered his wagon out of harm's way.

Following his lead, April drove the ATV to the far side of the road, but her float didn't maneuver well. It remained in the path of the charging horse. If the panicked animal veered around her float, it could trample someone on the still-crowded sidewalk. Jumping off the ATV, she tried dragging the float over as the horse bore down on her.

"April, *m-move!*"

His stutter galvanized her more than his command. She hurled herself over the float and landed on her hands and knees on the other side. He flashed by on the strawberry roan, threading the needle as only an expert rider in full control could do. Blood trickled from her arm where she'd gouged it on the side of the float. By the time she scrambled to her feet, Ryker had grabbed the runaway's bridle and pulled it to a halt. Somewhere along the way he'd lost his cap.

Immediately he turned toward her, his chest heaving. "Y-you okay?"

"Yes!" She stuck her arm behind her back so he wouldn't see that she was bleeding.

He dragged in another breath. "Stay put."

She nodded.

"Are you sure you're not hurt, April?" Zane rode up followed by the rest of the McGavins. "Looked like you took a tumble."

"Yes, but I'm fine." She ignored the sharp sting of torn flesh. "No worries."

Cody stood in his stirrups and peered into the wagon. "Mom? Ladies?"

"Everybody seems to be in good shape, Cody." Jim had climbed into the back and was checking them all.

"We're fine, Cody!" the women chorused.

"Well, good, then."

"Hey, Zane," Ryker called out. "Can you take charge of this animal?"

"Sure thing." Zane rode to meet him.

Ryker transferred control of the runaway to Zane and maneuvered his way back toward April. "Cody, Bryce, Trevor, you guys go down the line and see if anybody's hurt back there, like maybe the poor soul who got tossed off that horse."

"We're on it, big brother." Bryce led the way.

"I'll find out where the horse belongs," Zane said.

Ryker's expression was grim. "Not in a parade."

"Nope." Zane led the horse away.

April had never witnessed a military man in charge before, but the role suited Ryker to a tee. She couldn't let him see her arm, though, or he'd be humiliated in front of all these people.

He rode up and dismounted. "You sure nothing's wrong?"

"Nothing you need to worry about."

He took off his shades and tucked them in his jacket pocket. "Your arm's behind your back."

"It's nothing."

"It's bleeding, isn't it?"

"Ryker, go help your brothers. I'll handle this."

"What'd you cut it on?"

"Just the side of the float."

"So no rusty metal?"

"Nope."

He glanced up at the wagon. "Jim, you got a bandanna on you?"

"That I do." Jim walked to the back of the wagon and handed it over.

"Thanks. Let's see your arm, April."

"No."

"Trust me." His gaze was steady and his voice was calm.

All right, then. But she watched him closely to make sure he didn't topple over as she revealed the gash on her arm.

He didn't even flinch. Instead he carefully wrapped the bandanna around the wound and tied the ends. "That should hold you for the time being." Then he glanced at her. "Thanks for the hypnotherapy suggestion."

She gulped. "You're welcome."

"I'd better go check on my brothers." Putting on his shades, he swung into the saddle and trotted toward the back of the parade.

"I'll be damned."

April looked up at the sound of Kendra's voice. All the Whine and Cheese ladies were staring at Ryker as he rode away. Since they'd all known him forever, they'd be aware of his phobia.

Kendra looked down at April. "What's this about hypnotherapy?"

"I suggested he could try it, but he said it wouldn't work for him."

"Well, it seems that he changed his mind."

"Yes, it does." There was no way he'd done it to impress her. If this accident hadn't happened, she might never have known. He'd rid himself of his phobia so he could better serve others, and as luck would have it, she was the first one he'd had the opportunity to help. After all this time, she was beginning to understand what made him tick. The knowledge was humbling.

By some miracle no one had been seriously hurt during the episode. The shared disaster had bonded everyone more tightly than before and both marchers and spectators voted to continue the parade down to the park, which was mainly an open, grassy field. Today it provided plenty of room for floats, wagons, horses and people.

Everyone gathered in front of a platform that was erected every Labor Day and decorated with patriotic bunting. The flag Ryker had carried in the parade had been bolted into a metal base near the speaker's stand.

April sat on the grass and chatted with Mandy, Faith and the Whine and Cheese ladies. Appearing relaxed was a trick when Ryker stood with his brothers only a few feet away. Every time he laughed at one of their jokes or made a comment, she lost her place in the women's conversation.

The talking stopped when the high school band played *Stars and Stripes Forever*. Then the mayor, a statuesque woman in her fifties, gave a short welcome speech. "We'd hoped Ryker McGavin would consent to speak today," she said at the end of her prepared remarks. "That would be especially appropriate after this morning's events. But Ryker shuns the spotlight and he refused. His mom, however, wants to say a few words."

April glanced at Ryker and his brothers. Judging from their surprised expressions, none of them had known about this.

"Please give it up for Kendra McGavin, owner of Wild Creek Ranch."

Amid the applause, Kendra climbed the wooden steps, her chiffon belly dancing outfit rippling in the breeze. She took the mic. "I welcome this opportunity, because I have a story that will make you very proud of the fighting men and women of our country and especially one of our own."

Which could only be Ryker. He began quietly questioning his brothers, who all shook their heads as if they'd had no part in this. For their sake, April hoped they hadn't.

"Last June, my son Ryker was shot through the chest."

The crowd gasped.

"He thinks I don't know, and I might not have found out for some time. But I received a letter a few days ago." She held it up. "It's from the mother of Ryker's co-pilot, Aaron Donahue. I won't read you the whole thing, which describes in detail the night their F-15 Eagle went down behind enemy lines, an incident my son never mentioned, either."

April sat frozen, her heart aching for Ryker. He'd tried so hard to protect his mother from the reality of war.

Kendra paused to clear her throat. "Ryker had minor injuries but Aaron's leg was broken. And believe me, I know what that feels like. I can only imagine what this poor soldier was going through in the dark, with enemy forces closing in. Ryker radioed for a helicopter and hauled Aaron with him toward the rendezvous point. He had to light a flare to signal the helicopter, and just as it flew in, the enemy attacked. Ryker used himself as a shield to protect his injured co-pilot."

April closed her eyes. When she found the courage to look at Ryker, he'd bowed his head. He didn't want to relive this any more than she did.

"The helicopter crew was an elite unit that got them out before they were both killed. But here's the part of the letter I wanted you to hear. Maggie, Aaron's mother, says this: *Some people are born to be guardian angels. Your son is one of them.*" Kendra paused and her voice quivered. "I begged Ryker not to enlist. But now I know why he had to go, and Ryker, I promise that from this moment on, I will be stronger. I promise to be worthy of a son who has the courage to give his life for others."

In the silence that followed, April gulped and brushed at her cheeks. Then someone yelled, "Here's to Ryker McGavin!" Another cheer went up, and another and Ryker was mobbed. Kendra was mobbed, too. April stood so she could see what was happening on the platform. Eventually Ryker vaulted onto it and parted the crowd until he reached his mother. When he folded her in his arms, April lost it.

Years ago she'd accused him of being selfish, but she was the selfish one because she'd wanted to keep him to herself. He'd never belong to her, but maybe, if she hadn't ruined everything, he could belong *with* her.

She wouldn't get a chance to talk with him right now, though. He was surrounded by others and...wait a damn minute. Kendra had talked about being worthy of Ryker's nobility. To be worthy of a man like Ryker, a person had to have gumption.

She had gumption! She'd been president of a champion debate team. And she was hopelessly in love with the man in the dark blue uniform. Time to tell him so.

A portion of the crowd seemed to be moving in the direction of the Guzzling Grizzly even though it wasn't yet noon. Didn't matter. Everyone wanted to buy Ryker a drink. She raced to her float, unhooked her ATV and hopped on. The zippy little machine got her to the bar a little ahead of the foot traffic.

Bryce had beat her there. He glanced up when she came in. "Hey, April! How's it going?"

"Bryce, I hate to bother you, but I need your help."

He continued stacking clean mugs behind the bar. "I'll do my best, but things are a little hectic with my big brother being the hero of the hour and half the town about to descend on this establishment."

"I only need two things and then I'll be out of your hair. Do you have a first aid kit?"

"I do." He paused to look at her with concern. "Sorry. I'm a butthead. I forgot you were hurt earlier. Let's go get it." He came out from behind the bar.

"Just tell me where it is."

"Easier if I just grab it for you." He started toward his office. "How's your arm?"

She fell into step beside him. "It'll be fine, especially if you have some antiseptic and a butterfly bandage."

"Got both. This is a bar. Stuff happens." He opened his office door and ushered her inside.

She evaluated the Spartan room. Not a very romantic rendezvous spot but it would have to do.

"Your office is the second favor. Could I please borrow it?"

"For what?" He crossed to a closet.

"I'd like a private place to talk with Ryker. I'll just stay here, if you wouldn't mind asking him to come find me."

"All right." He pulled a first aid kit out of a closet and handed it to her. "Need any help with the bandaging?"

"I can do it. Thanks, Bryce. You'd better go tend bar."

"I'll send him in."

"Thank you." After he left she used an antiseptic wipe to clean her wound, applied some antibacterial salve, and put on a bandage. Then she sat in Bryce's desk chair to wait.

When Ryker walked through the door, she got up. "Thanks for coming."

"N-no problem." His expression was stern, almost belligerent. "Bryce said he hauled out the f-first aid kit for you. I'm glad you asked h-him for it."

She was transfixed by his stammer. Had the letter from Aaron's mom stirred up a nightmare of memories?

"What d-did you want to s-see me about?"

Our future. But she hesitated to blurt that out when he was clearly stressed. "That was some story."

His gaze bored into her. "And you h-hated it."

"No more than you, I'm sure."

"It was a b-bad night. If I'd s-seen my own blood, Aaron was a g-goner."

"*Aaron* was a goner? What about you?"

He shrugged. "It'd be my own d-damn fault. But Aaron was c-counting on me."

She rounded the desk. "And you saved him. It's over."

"N-no, it's not."

"Yes, it is, Ryker." She laid a hand on his arm. "But it looks as if that letter brought it all back, and now you're reliving—"

"Not m-me! You!"

"Me?" She stared at him in astonishment. "I wasn't even there!"

"B-but now you will be. Every time you l-look at me, you'll think of it! That's what you wanted to t-talk about, right? And now we're d-done!" His expression clouded with what looked like fury.

Only it wasn't fury. Heart pounding, she gazed into blue eyes that had turned almost black with fear. "That isn't why I needed to see you. I wanted a private place to tell you that I love you more than I ever thought possible. And if you can forgive me for being an idiot, I—"

"G-good God." He stared at her for a long moment. Then, with a groan, he swept her up, almost crushing her. "There's n-nothing to forgive." He pulled her closer, holding her tight against his big body. "I've n-never loved any other woman. Just you."

Steel bands of anxiety loosened, making room for a rush of gratitude. Angry words and years apart hadn't extinguished that tender flame. She was blessed.

Slowly he relaxed his grip and his gaze met hers. Hope gradually replaced the dark fear in his eyes. "Are you...are you saying we can make this work?"

"Yes." She swallowed. "It seems I can't live without you."

"Oh, April." He kissed her, hard at first, and then more gently, until he slowly lifted his head. "I thought I'd lost you."

Her heart swelled with compassion. "Well, you haven't. I'm right here and now you'll never get rid of me."

"Best news ever." He glanced around the office and took a shaky breath. "Hell of a place to make love, though."

"Especially with all those people out there. Shouldn't you—"

"No. I hate this hero stuff. I warned Bryce I'd be making an early exit."

"Unfortunately my ATV's out front."

His mouth tilted up. "But my horse is out back."

"No kidding?"

"A good soldier always has an exit strategy."

Giddy with love, she was ready for anything. "Now I really feel like Snow White."

He cupped her face and placed butterfly kisses all over it. "How's that?"

"I'm wide awake and I get a second chance to nab Prince Charming."

"Hey, I'm not—"

"Yes, you are, cowboy." She gazed into his eyes. "But if you want to stop me from heaping praise on your heroic self, you can always kiss me again. You're the best kisser I know."

He leaned down, his warm breath tickling her mouth. "And then what?"

"We'll ride off on your fast horse and make wild and crazy love for the rest of the day and into the night."

"I like it. We might even find inner peas."

"We just might." As his mouth settled over hers, her world made sense at last. She was where she was supposed to be. In Ryker's arms.

Bryce McGavin's broken heart dances a two-step when he meets songbird Nicole Williams in A COWBOY'S HEART, book four in the McGavin Brothers series!

* * * * *

Bryce was almost finished wiping down the liquor bottles lining the glass shelves when Nicole came through the door, a guitar case in her hand.

She walked up to the bar and set the case on the floor before perching on a stool. "Hi."

His heartbeat sped up, most likely because he hadn't expected her. "Hey." He tossed down the bar rag. "Nice to see you again." He should ask about the guitar but he was too busy looking at her and regulating his breathing.

"I should have called in advance, but I was afraid you'd turn me down, so I just drove over."

"Turn you down for what?" Considering her recent engagement and her attack cat, he was way too excited that she was here.

She looked younger today. Maybe it was the freckles he hadn't noticed before, or it could be her hair. He was used to seeing it tamed into undulating waves, but today it fell to her shoulders in a mass of ringlets as if she'd washed it and let it air dry.

She took a deep breath. "I'd like to play at the Guzzling Grizzly."

"But we already have a—"

"I don't mean on Friday and Saturday nights. You need dance bands for that crowd, but maybe Sunday and Monday night would work."

"What kind of music?"

"I specialize in country, but I can handle the occasional folk song and some classic rock tunes. I performed two nights a week in Idaho Falls at a place called Trail's End Tavern." The tremble in her voice was slight, but it was enough to betray her nervousness. "It was a little smaller than this. I can give you the owner's name and number if you'd like to contact him."

"That won't be necessary." He admired her courage. He'd never been in her shoes, never had to work up the nerve to ask for a job playing guitar. Lou had recruited him at the tender age of seventeen. "I wish I could give you an answer, but the owner's been booking our entertainment. Before I can say yes or no, I'll have to check with him and see if he's willing to add more nights to the schedule. It might not be in the budget."

"You wouldn't have to pay me. I'll work for tips."

"Um, okay." Warning bells clanged. Often people willing to perform for free were lousy musicians. He wouldn't have to consult with Lou if he didn't have to pay her, but he should find out if she was any good before he turned her loose on his customers. If she sucked, then he'd have the crummy job of rejecting her.

"I brought my guitar hoping I could audition this afternoon. For all you know, I sound like a pack of coyotes after a rabbit."

"I'm sure you don't." He knew no such thing. "But since you brought your guitar, might as well play something for me."

"I was hoping you'd say that." Hopping off the stool, she opened the case and lifted out a black guitar.

He got a load of that instrument and came around from behind the bar lickity-split. "You play a RainSong?" The expensive graphite guitars fascinated him. They were practically immune to either dampness or extremely dry air. What a crying shame if she was a rank amateur who owned a primo instrument, but it happened.

"You know the brand?"

"Sure do. Thought about getting one. But the price for a lefty was more than I could afford."

She blinked. "You play?"

"Not currently."

"I guess managing the bar keeps you pretty busy."

"It does and I...I just lost interest."

Her eyes held a question.

He shrugged. "People change."

"Some do." She waited as if giving him time to say more. When he didn't, she hoisted the guitar strap over her shoulder. "Let's get 'er done." She crossed to the stage and perched on one of several stools left there for the band.

"Want a mic?"

"Not unless you want me to use one."

"Not necessary. I'll sit close." He walked over to a table in front and pulled out a chair.

She settled the guitar in her lap. "This is one of my favorites from the Statler Brothers, *Flowers on the Wall.*"

He scrubbed a hand over his face to hide his dismay. The beloved old tune was one of his favorites, too, but he wouldn't have chosen it for an audition. It was growing moss. He began dreaming up gentle ways to tell her she wouldn't be performing at the GG.

He hated the idea of crushing her hopes when she looked so cute sitting on that stool with her wild hair and her fancy guitar, but as the manager he had a duty to—*holy crap*. The woman could sing.

And play. That RainSong came alive under her fingers. As she romped through the silly lyrics, he tapped his foot in time with the beat and caught himself smiling.

She met his gaze and smiled back.

As if he'd grabbed onto a live wire, the air whooshed from his lungs. His ears started buzzing and his chest grew tight. Damn! He'd decided weeks ago to steer clear of this woman and the same reasons still applied.

He managed to get himself back together as she finished up and slid off the stool. He stood and his shaky legs held him. Excellent. She'd never guess that she'd just rocked his world with the combo of her music and that smile.

The couple from Massachusetts clapped enthusiastically and she gave them a quick bow before turning back to him. "It was okay?"

"More than okay." He cleared his throat. "I'd very much like you to play on Sunday and Monday nights."

She pumped a fist. "Booyah!"

He couldn't remember the last time he'd made someone that happy. If seeing her perform twice a week caused him to want things he couldn't have, he'd deal with it. "When would you like to start?"

She put her guitar away. "How about tonight?"

"Works for me."

"Will you be here?" She glanced up, her expression open and excited.

"Yep. How's six o'clock sound?"

"Perfect. I can feed Jimi and pop on over."

"Jimi's doing okay?"

"Never better."

"Have you heard from—"

"No."

"Good."

Picking up her guitar case, Nicole gave him a little wave. "See you at six!"

"Looking forward to it." Truer words were never spoken, which made him officially pathetic.

New York Times bestselling author Vicki Lewis Thompson's love affair with cowboys started with the Lone Ranger, continued through Maverick, and took a turn south of the border with Zorro. She views cowboys as the Western version of knights in shining armor, rugged men who value honor, honesty and hard work. Fortunately for her, she lives in the Arizona desert, where broad-shouldered, lean-hipped cowboys abound. Blessed with such an abundance of inspiration, she only hopes that she can do them justice.

For more information about this prolific author, visit her website and sign up for her newsletter. She loves connecting with readers.

VickiLewisThompson.com

CPSIA information can be obtained
at www.ICGtesting.com
Printed in the USA
LVOW12s0315191117
556876LV00001B/5/P